Editor
Sarah Beatty

Editorial Project Manager
Mara Ellen Guckian

Editor-in-Chief
Sharon Coan, M.S. Ed.

Illustrator
Alexandra Artigas

Cover Artist
Barb Lorseyedi

Art Coordinator
Kevin Barnes

Art Director
Cjae Froshay

Imaging
James Edward Grace
Rosa C. See

Product Manager
Phil Garcia

Publishers
Rachelle Cracchiolo, M.S. Ed.
Mary Dupuy Smith, M.S. Ed.

Skill Builders for Young Learners
Beginning Reading
Early Childhood

Authors

Tracy Jarboe & Stefani Sadler, M.A.

Teacher Created Materials, Inc.
6421 Industry Way
Westminster, CA 92683
www.teachercreated.com
ISBN-0-7439-3688-4

©2002 Teacher Created Materials, Inc.
Made in U.S.A.

The classroom teacher may reproduce copies of materials in this book for classroom use only. The reproduction of any part for an entire school or school system is strictly prohibited. No part of this publication may be transmitted, stored, or recorded in any form without written permission from the publisher.

Table of Contents

Introduction................... 3
**Development of
Foundational Skills**........... 4
How to Use This Book........ 5
Motor Skill Development
    Going Home................. 6
    Shapes..................... 7
    Fun with Cutting............ 8
    Sammy Snake.............. 9
    I Can Print My Name........ 10
Matching
    Time to Eat!................ 11
    School Fun................. 12
Left and Right
    Fun with Left and Right..... 13
    Left and Right.............. 14
Patterns
    Fun with Fruit.............. 15
    Bugs, Bugs, Bugs........... 16
    Fun with Pattern Cards...... 17
    Ladybug Cards............. 18
    Fish Cards................. 19
    Duck Cards................ 20
Sequencing
    From Seed to Flower........ 21
    Build a Snowman........... 22
Alphabet
    My Alphabet Book.......... 23
    Fish Flashcard Games....... 37
    Fish Flashcards............ 38

Alphabet Review
    Letter Cheer................ 44
    I Can Print the Alphabet..... 45
    Find the Clown
    (Lowercase Dot-to-Dot)...... 46
    Alpha-Bear
    (Uppercase Dot-to-Dot)...... 47
Phonemic Awareness
    I Hear . . . (Letter Sounds).... 48
    Beginning Sounds.......... 74
    What's Missing?............ 77
    What Am I?................ 78
    Ending Sounds............. 79
    Sound Matching & Sound
    Isolation................... 81
    Sound Blending & Sound
    Substitution................ 82
Syllabication
    What Do You Hear?......... 83
Rhyme
    Find the Rhyme............. 84
    Fun with Rhymes........... 85
Sentence Building
    I Can Read................. 87
Reading
    Color Word Book........... 89
    Number Word Book......... 94

Introduction

There are many essential elements to a balanced pre-reading program that can be easily integrated across the curriculum and practiced throughout the day. Research and practice have shown that children learn best when they are surrounded by meaningful environmental print in an engaging atmosphere of learning. This is a classroom where children are read to often and where they are given opportunities to engage in activities designed to foster a genuine understanding of concepts in print.

Reading to young children several times each day is critical, as children need to:

- see teachers model the reading process
- hear the words and sounds
- notice rhythms and patterns
- discern vocal intonations and inflections
- enjoy quality literature

This process allows children to experience more complex language structures, story lines, and character development. The class discussions that follow a story time provide an opportunity for students to access higher level critical thinking skills.

Skill Builders for Young Learners: Beginning Reading is designed to facilitate the teaching of basic pre-reading skills through the use of activity-based worksheets. The pre-reading skills addressed include fine motor skill development, matching, patterning, left-to-right directionality, sequencing, letter recognition and formation, consonant and vowel sound usage, visual discrimination, and phonemic awareness.

Activity pages can be completed easily, using crayons, pencils, scissors, and glue. Each activity is designed to give students practice with a specific reading-readiness skill while simultaneously enhancing fine motor skill development through coloring, tracing, cutting, and pasting.

Activities in this book have been placed in a sequence that scaffolds the learning process but may be used in whatever manner best matches your curricular scope and sequence.

Development of Foundational Skills

In recent years, many states have been adopting more rigorous content standards and frameworks for reading and mathematics instruction for kindergarten. This greatly increases the need for more challenging pre-school readiness programs designed to meet the requirements for today's children. Children are expected to enter kindergarten better prepared for new learning and possessing skills once attributed to 1st or 2nd grade. The activities in this book are specifically designed to enhance instructional practice in the benchmarked pre-kindergarten skill development areas.

The following list is a synthesis of the standards, benchmarks, and skills, similar to the ones required by your state and school district.

- Knows (some) letter names.
- Knows (some) letter sounds.
- Understands that letters make up words.
- Knows the letters needed to spell one's own name.
- Knows basic colors, shapes and numbers to 10.
- Demonstrates read-like behaviors, such as pretending to read and write.
- Recognizes print in the environment.
- Distinguishes separate words.
- Can break one syllable words into phonemes (C-A-T).
- Can blend phonemes to make a word.
- Can recognize all objects that begin with a specific sound.
- Recognizes rhyming words.
- Demonstrates an understanding of picture books and simple stories.
- Retells stories, makes predictions, and connects stories to background experiences in a teacher-guided group format.

How to Use This Book

The activities and lessons in *Skill Builders for Young Learners: Beginning Reading* are intended for children aged 3–6. They may be used for small group or total class instruction, depending on the age and independence level of the students. Every effort has been made to design effective, motivating activities that will encourage pre-reading skills. Each activity is developmentally appropriate and will be instrumental in building a foundation for reading readiness.

Reproducible worksheets are provided with simple directions for use. The icons on each worksheet enable students to gather materials easily. These worksheets require only the use of common classroom supplies such as pencils, scissors, crayons and glue. Letters and letter sounds are referred to often. A letter name is preceded and ended with quotation marks, "m." A slash before and after a letter, /m/, indicates the letter sound *mmmmmm*, not "m."

It is always advisable to carefully model each step of an activity to ensure student success. Patterns may be used to produce overhead transparencies for total class lesson presentation. This lesson could then be followed by independent seatwork where students would complete the same activity on their own pages.

An award certificate is included below to recognize achievement. Praise and recognition of skill mastery encourage students to be self-motivated and gain confidence necessary to attempt new skills.

Congratulations!

You did a wonderful job on

_____

Date   *Teacher*

Motor Skill Development

 a b c d e f g h i j k l m n o p q r s t u v w x y z

Going Home

 Trace from left to right using "rainbow tracing." Use several different color crayons to trace over the lines.

 Color the pictures.

Motor Skill Development

a b c d e f g h i j k l m n o p q r s t u v w x y z

Shapes

 Trace these shapes and then color them.

Triangles have three lines,

Put them together, three corners you'll find.

Four straight lines all the same,

Put them together and square is the name.

A circle always curves around,

No beginning or end can be found.

A rectangle has four lines in all,

Two are short and two are tall.

You see them here,
You see them there,
Basic shapes are everywhere.
Can you find each of these shapes in your classroom?

©Teacher Created Materials, Inc.   7   #3688 Skill Builders: Beginning Reading

Motor Skill Development

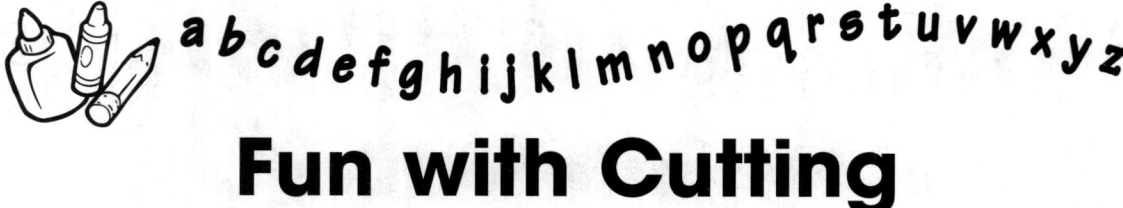

Fun with Cutting

✂ Cut on each of the lines moving from the left to the right.

✂ --

✂ --

✂ Cut along angled lines by stopping at each point and changing directions.

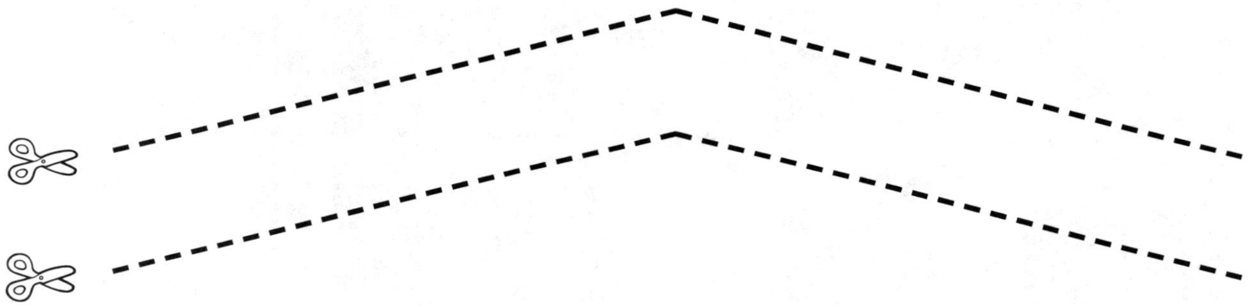

✂
✂

✂ Cut with one hand while turning the paper with the other.

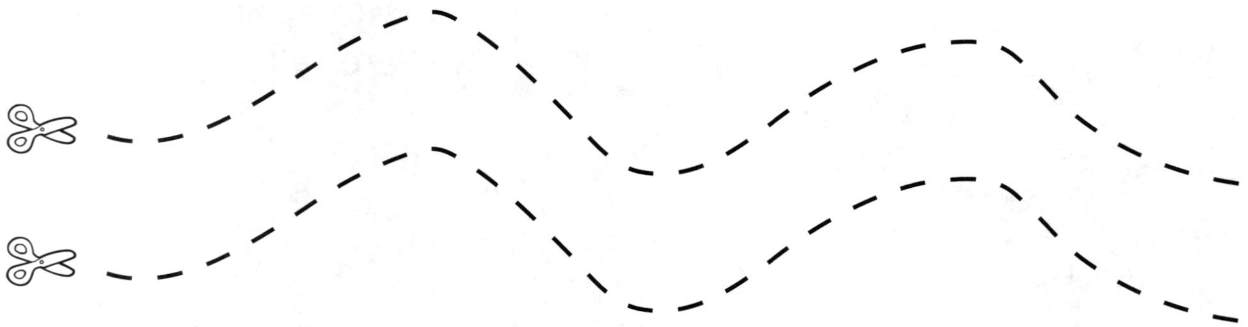

✂
✂

Motor Skill Development

a b c d e f g h i j k l m n o p q r s t u v w x y z

Sammy Snake

 Make Sammy Snake by cutting on the dotted line.

 For fun, color your snake and tie a string on the end of your snake so that you can hang it up.

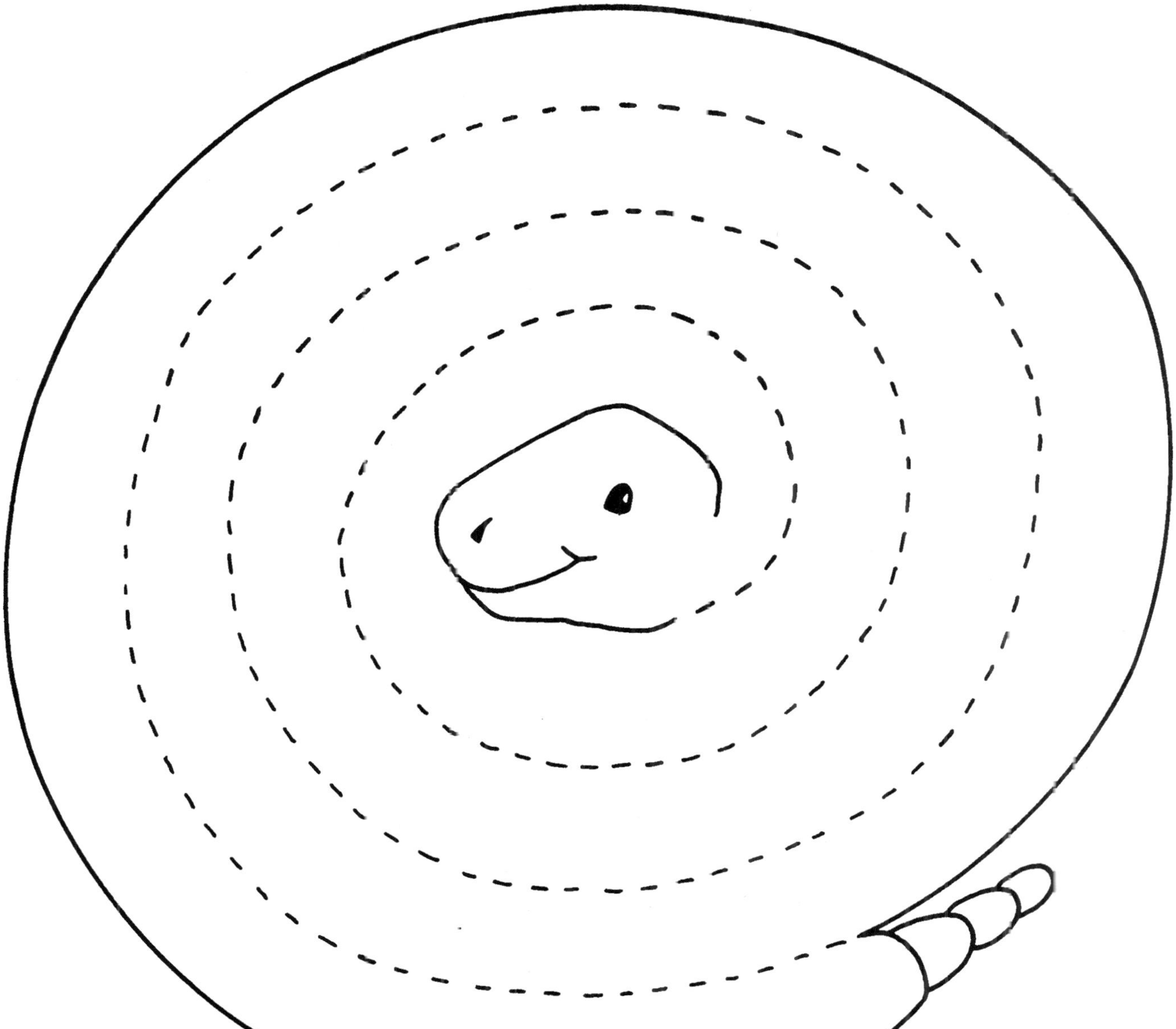

Motor Skill Development

abcdefghijklmnopqrstuvwxyz

I Can Print My Name

After your teacher has written your name on the line, trace over it with rainbow writing. Then try writing it yourself.

Here are some ideas to try at home:

1. Make your name using play dough, magnetic letters, foam letters, alphabet cereal or alphabet cookies.
2. Write your name using crayon or markers. Cut your name apart letter by letter. Can you put your name back together? Save your name puzzle pieces in a resealable bag.
3. Use a small amount of sand or salt to fill a cookie tray. Then practice printing your name in the sand or salt using your index finger.

Matching

a b c d e f g h i j k l m n o p q r s t u v w x y z

Time to Eat!

 Draw a line from each object on the left to the matching object on the right.

©Teacher Created Materials, Inc. #3688 Skill Builders: Beginning Reading

Matching

 abcdefghijklmnopqrstuvwxyz

School Fun

 Draw a line from each object on the left to the matching object on the right.

#3688 Skill Builders: Beginning Reading   12   ©Teacher Created Materials, Inc.

Left and Right

a b c d e f g h i j k l m n o p q r s t u v w x y z
Fun with Left and Right

 Use purple to color the flower on the right and blue to color the flower on the left.

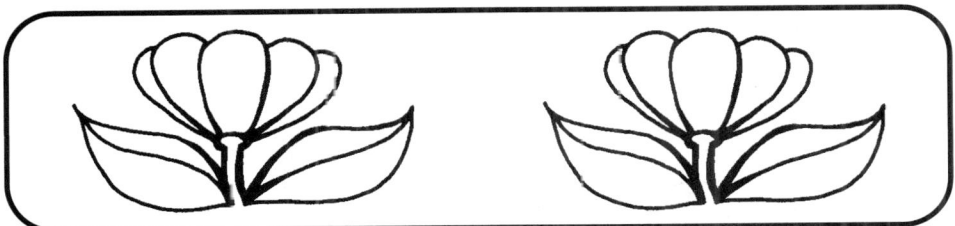

 Use green to color the apple on the right and red to color the apple on the left.

 Use orange to color the fish on the right and yellow to color the fish on the left.

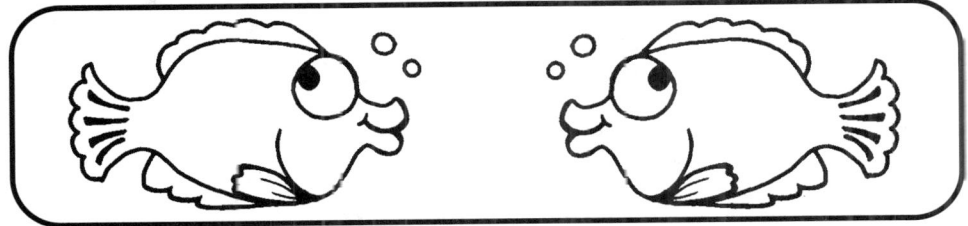

Here are some ideas to try at home:

1. Have an exercise time with your child. Give clear directions such as these: Hop on your right foot. Touch your left toe. Jump to the right. Stretch your left hand to the sky.
2. When putting on socks and shoes, begin with the left foot and then the right.
3. Using a cosmetic pencil, place the letter "R" on top of your child's right hand and the letter "L" on top of the left hand. Ask your child to do things throughout the day specifying right or left. Use the letters as a guide.

Left and Right

 a b c d e f g h i j k l m n o p q r s t u v w x y z

Left and Right

 Use brown to color the bear on the right and black to color the bear on the left.

 Use yellow to color the sun on the left and orange to color the sun on the right.

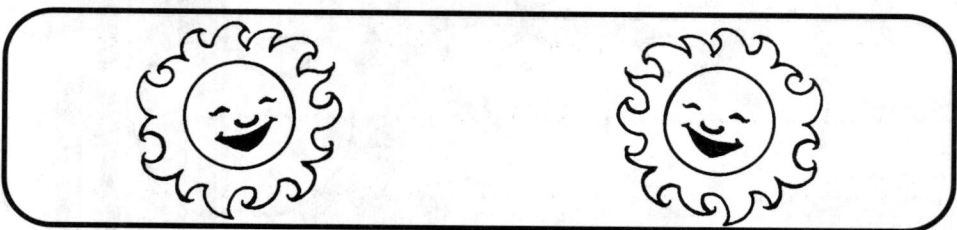

 Use red to color the bird on the right and blue to color the bird on the left.

Here are some ideas to try at home:

1. Have your child help you set the table. Give verbal directions such as these: Place the fork on the left and the spoon on the right. Place the napkin on the right and the glass on the left.

2. Play a directionality game. Give verbal directions to move your child from one place to the other. For example: Take eight steps to the right. Now take four steps straight ahead to the kitchen. Now take six steps to the left to the kitchen counter. What do you see? Homemade cookies just for you and me!

Patterns

abcdefghijklmnopqrstuvwxyz

Fun with Fruit

 Look at the pattern below. Color the pictures.

 Cut out the pictures at the bottom of the page.

 Glue the pictures in the same order as the pattern.

©Teacher Created Materials, Inc. #3688 Skill Builders: Beginning Reading

Patterns

Bugs, Bugs, Bugs

 Look at the pattern below. Color the pictures.

 Cut out the pictures at the bottom of the page.

 Glue the pictures in the same order as the pattern.

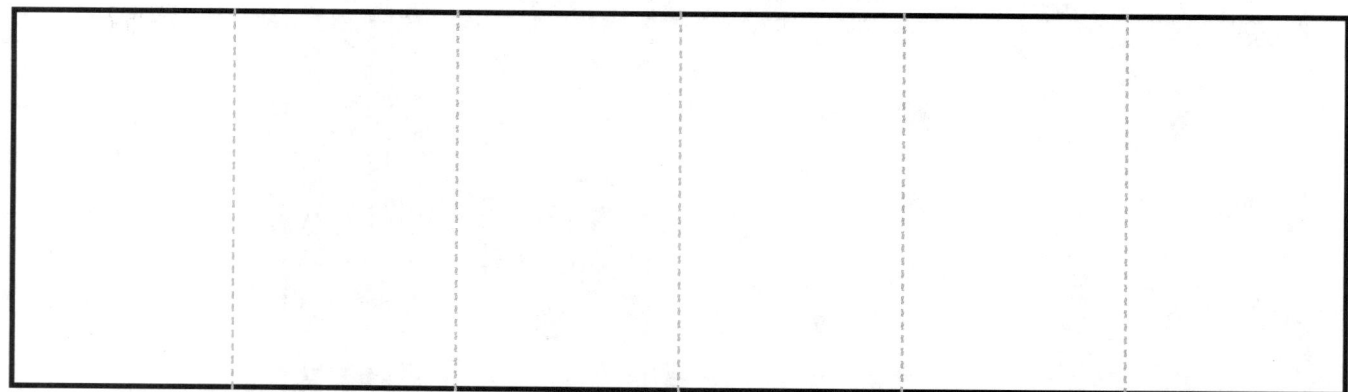

Patterns

a b c d e f g h i j k l m n o p q r s t u v w x y z
Fun with Pattern Cards

Teacher: Copy the following pattern card pages (18–20) onto heavy construction paper or tag. Have the students color the pictures and cut them apart. Have the students make a pattern using the pictures.

The pattern can be placed on the floor, in a pocket chart, or mounted onto poster board strips. An example would be—bear, bear, ladybug, duck, bear, bear, ladybug, duck, bear, bear, ladybug, duck, and so on.

You can make the patterns more complex by copying the characters onto different colors of construction paper. For example: green ladybug, yellow ladybug, brown bear, green duck, green ladybug, yellow ladybug, brown bear, green duck, green ladybug, yellow ladybug, brown bear, green duck. What two patterns are represented here? Besides the AABC, AABC, AABC critter pattern, there is also a color pattern.

Patterns

 abcdefghijklmnopqrstuvwxyz

Ladybug Cards

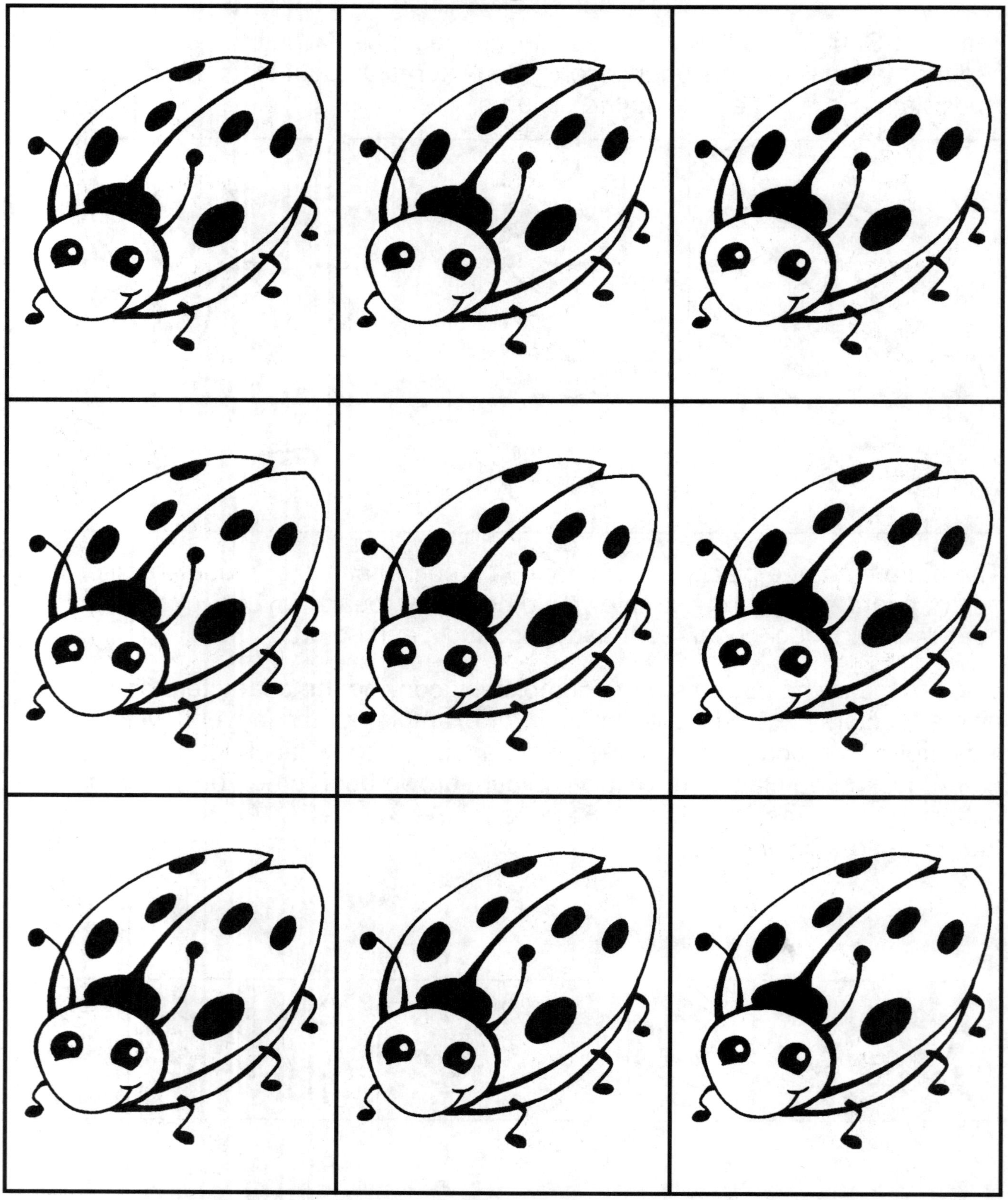

abcdefghijklmnopqrstuvwxyz

Patterns

Fish Cards

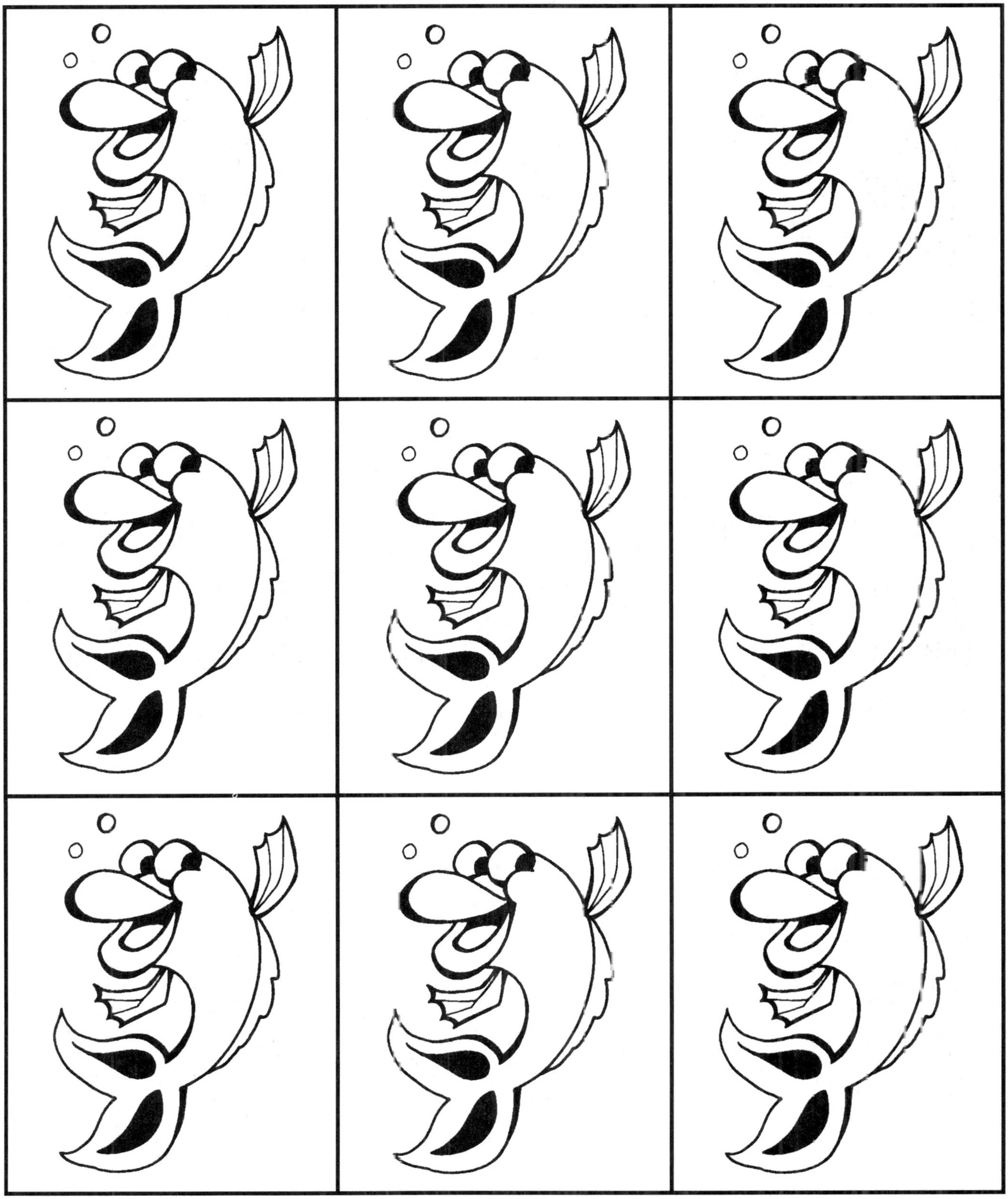

Patterns

 abcdefghijklmnopqrstuvwxyz

Duck Cards

#3688 Skill Builders: Beginning Reading 20 ©Teacher Created Materials, Inc.

Sequencing

abcdefghijklmnopqrstuvwxyz
From Seed to Flower

 Color the pictures.

 Cut out the 4 pictures and arrange them in order.

 Glue the pictures onto a strip of construction paper in the correct sequence or staple them together to make a book.

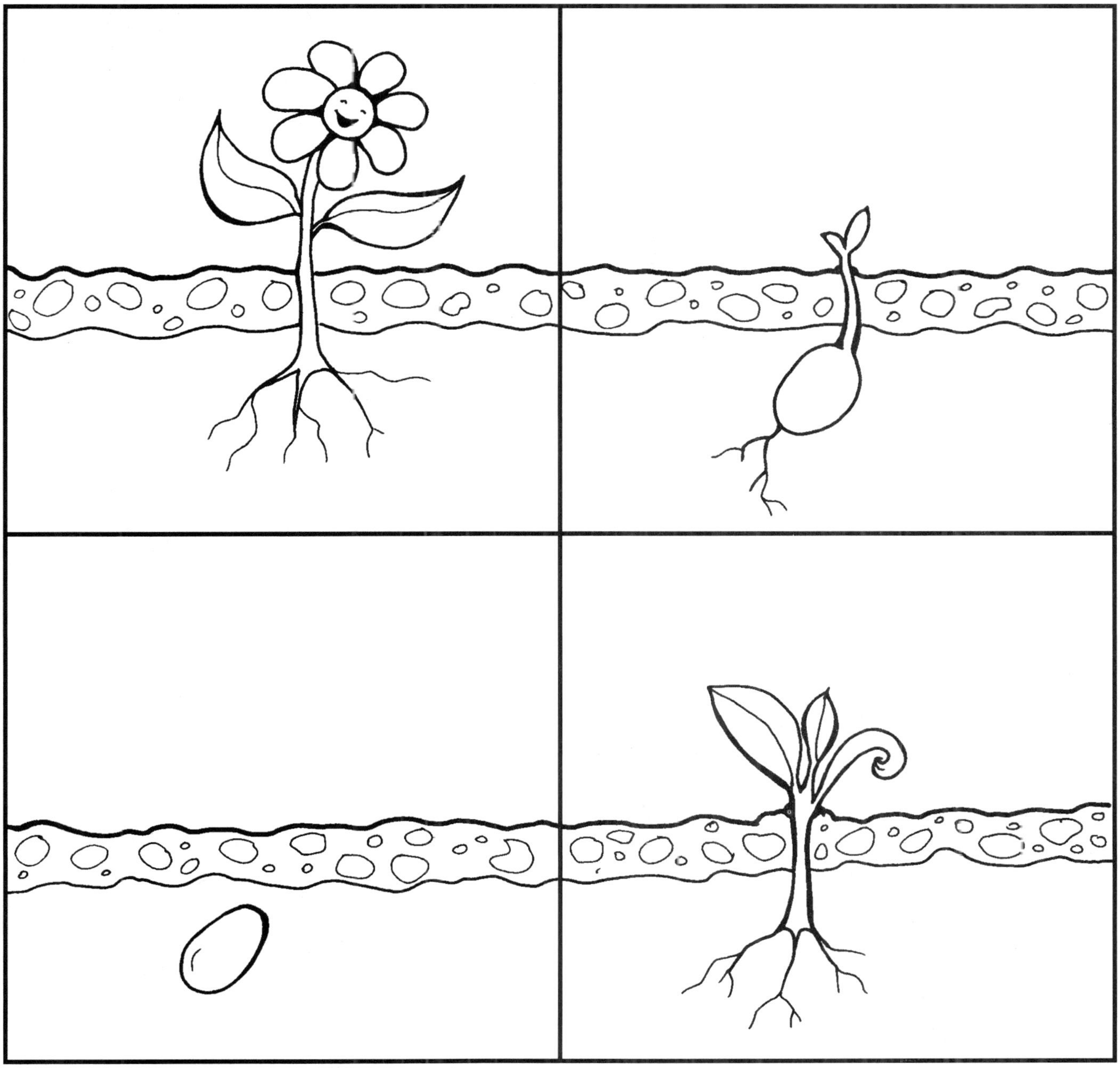

Sequencing

 abcdefghijklmnopqrstuvwxyz

Build a Snowman

 Color the pictures.

 Cut out the 6 pictures and arrange them in order.

 Glue the pictures onto a long strip of construction paper in the correct sequence or staple them together to make a book.

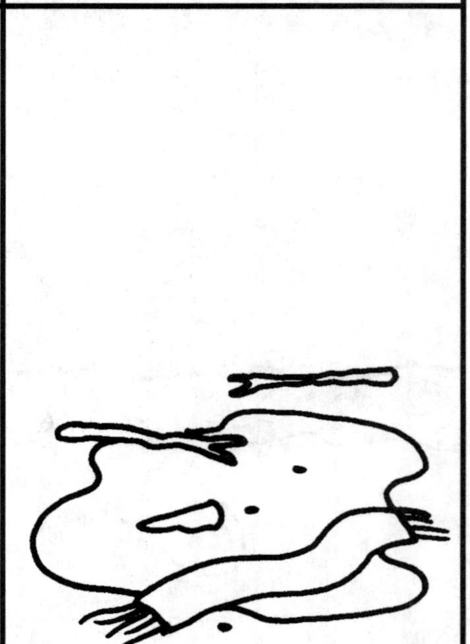

My Alphabet Book

Pages 24–36 can be used as individual worksheets or combined to form an alphabet review for students. To create the alphabet book, have students complete the following steps for each page.

1. Cut out the page on the dashed lines.
2. Trace the letter and then draw two more letters.
3. Circle all the uppercase letters in the picture with a crayon.
4. Circle all the lowercase letters in the picture with a different color crayon.
5. Color the picture.

To assemble the alphabet book, have students complete the following steps.

1. Cut out and decorate the cover below.
2. Arrange the pages in alphabetical order.
3. Place the decorated cover on top of the alphabet pages.
4. Staple the pages together.

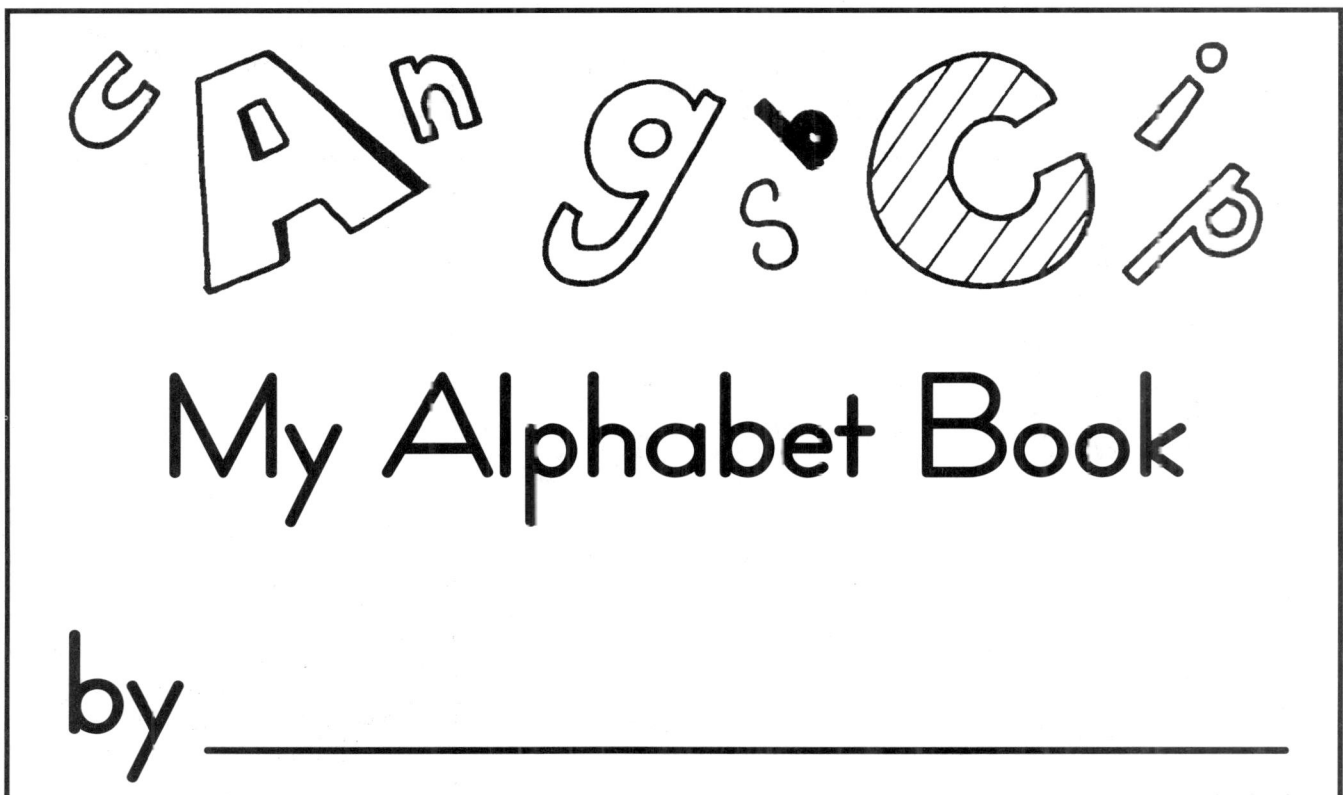

Alphabet

 abcdefghijklmnopqrstuvwxyz

Aa is for apple.

A   a

Bb is for balloon.

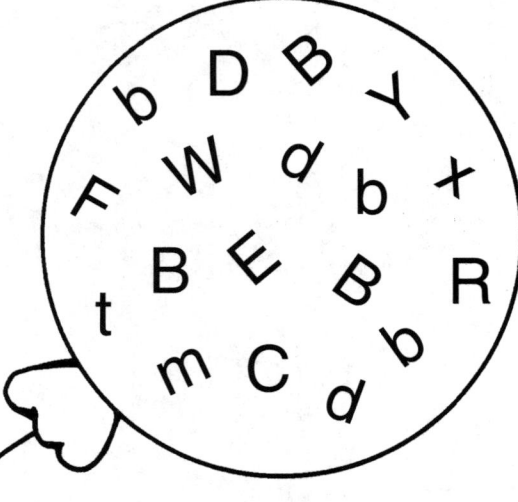

B   b

Alphabet

a b c d e f g h i j k l m n o p q r s t u v w x y z

Cc is for cap.

C   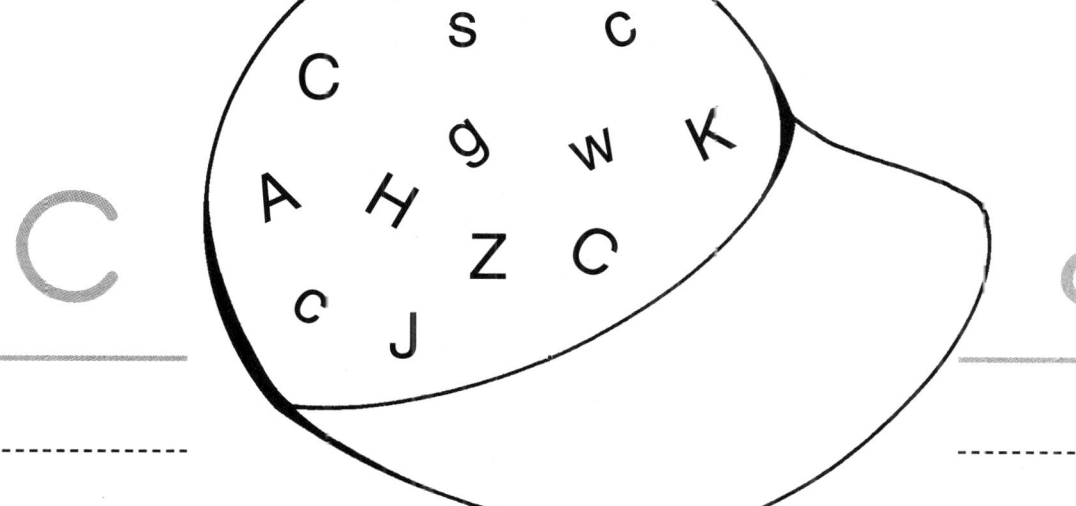   c

Dd is for dinosaur.

D      d

Alphabet

 a b c d e f g h i j k l m n o p q r s t u v w x y z

Ee is for egg.

E   e

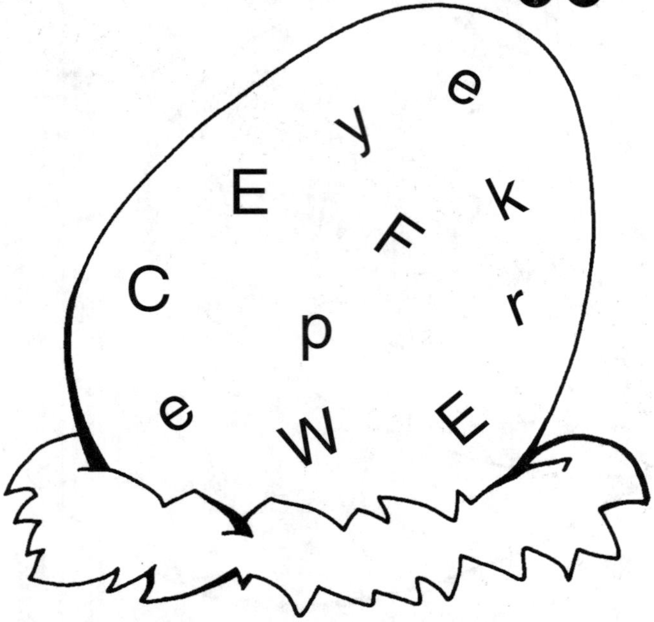

Ff is for fish.

F   f

Alphabet

a b c d e f g h i j k l m n o p q r s t u v w x y z

Gg is for guitar.

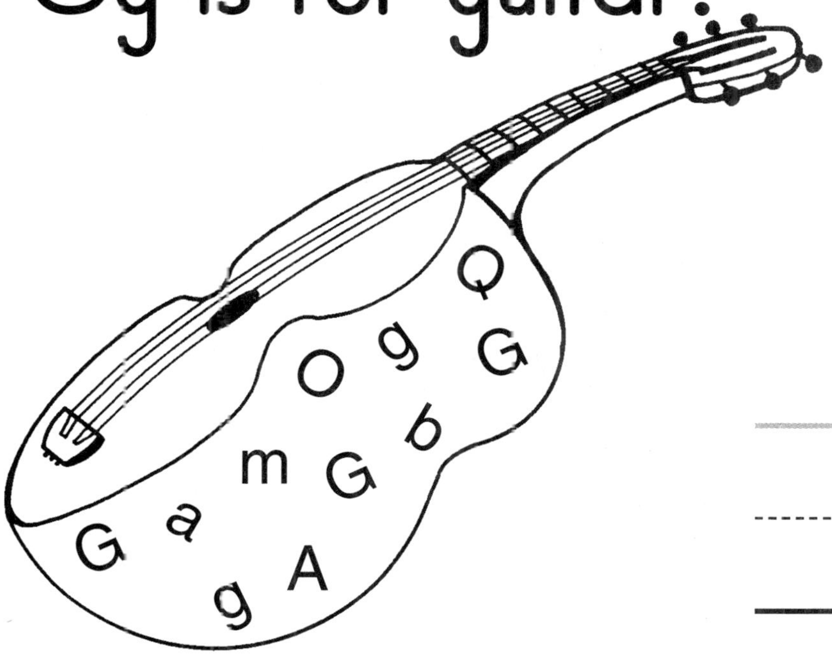

G   g

Hh is for heart.

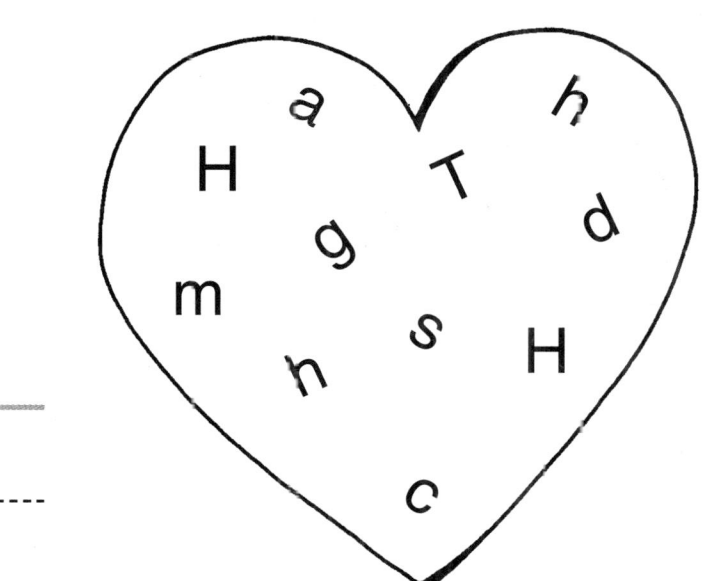

H   h

Alphabet

abcdefghijklmnopqrstuvwxyz

Ii is for igloo.

I   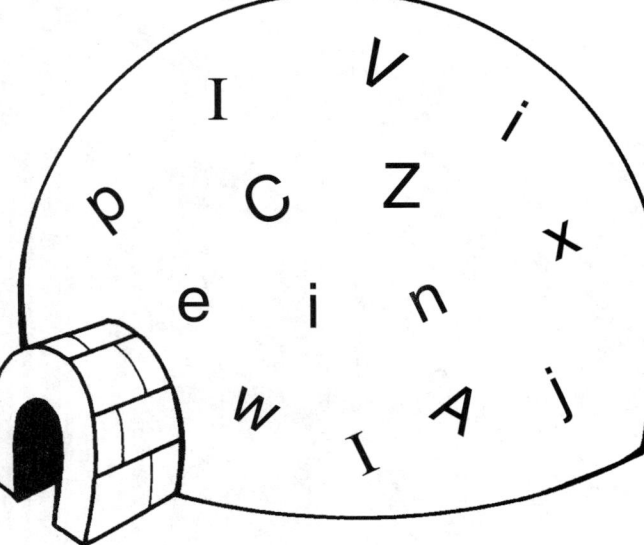   i

Jj is for jar.

J      j

Alphabet

a b c d e f g h i j k l m n o p q r s t u v w x y z

Kk is for kite.

K   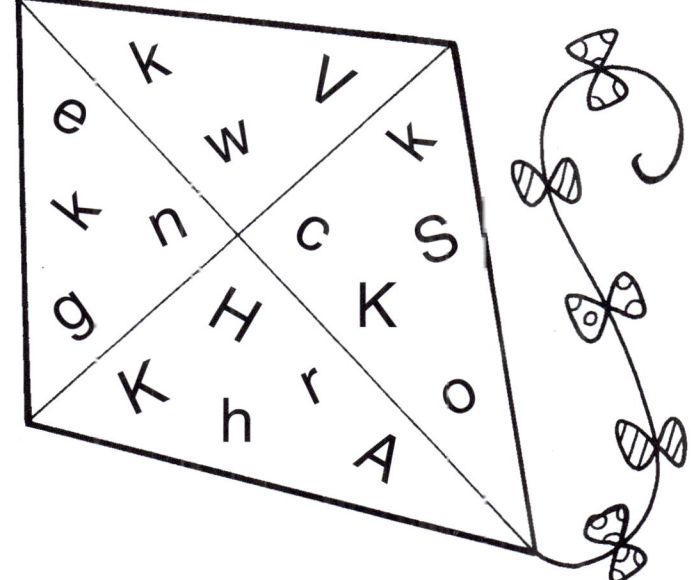   k

Ll is for lamp.

L   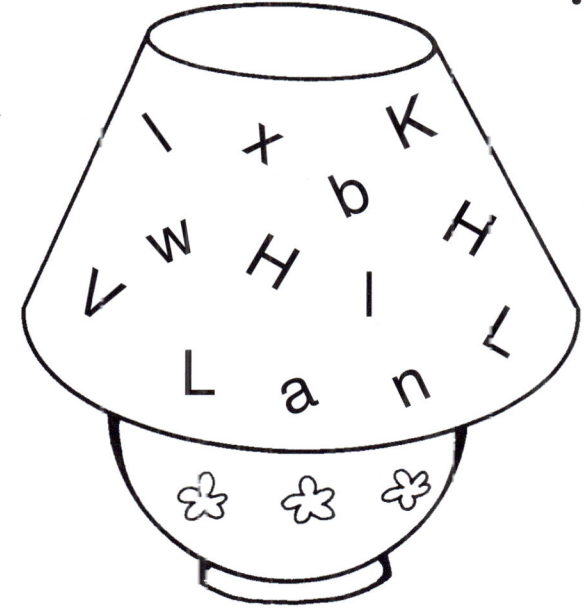   l

Alphabet

abcdefghijklmnopqrstuvwxyz

Mm is for mitten.

M 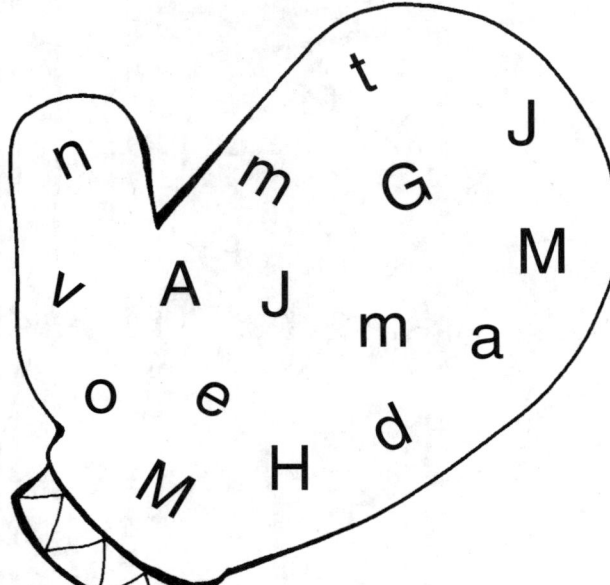 m

Nn is for napkin.

N 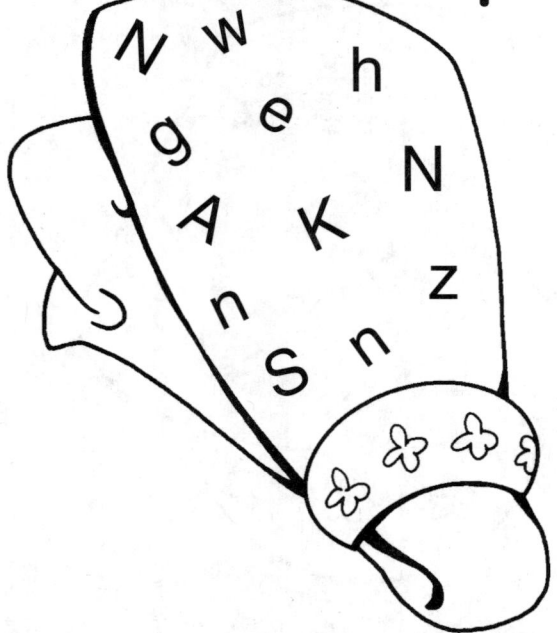 n

Alphabet

a b c d e f g h i j k l m n o p q r s t u v w x y z

Oo is for olive.

O 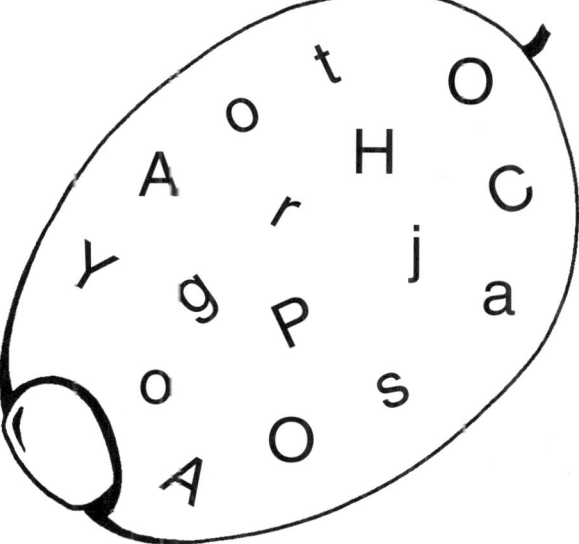 o

Pp is for pumpkin.

P  p

Alphabet

 a b c d e f g h i j k l m n o p q r s t u v w x y z

Qq is for quilt.

Q   q

Rr is for rabbit.

R   r

Alphabet

abcdefghijklmnopqrstuvwxyz

Ss is for star.

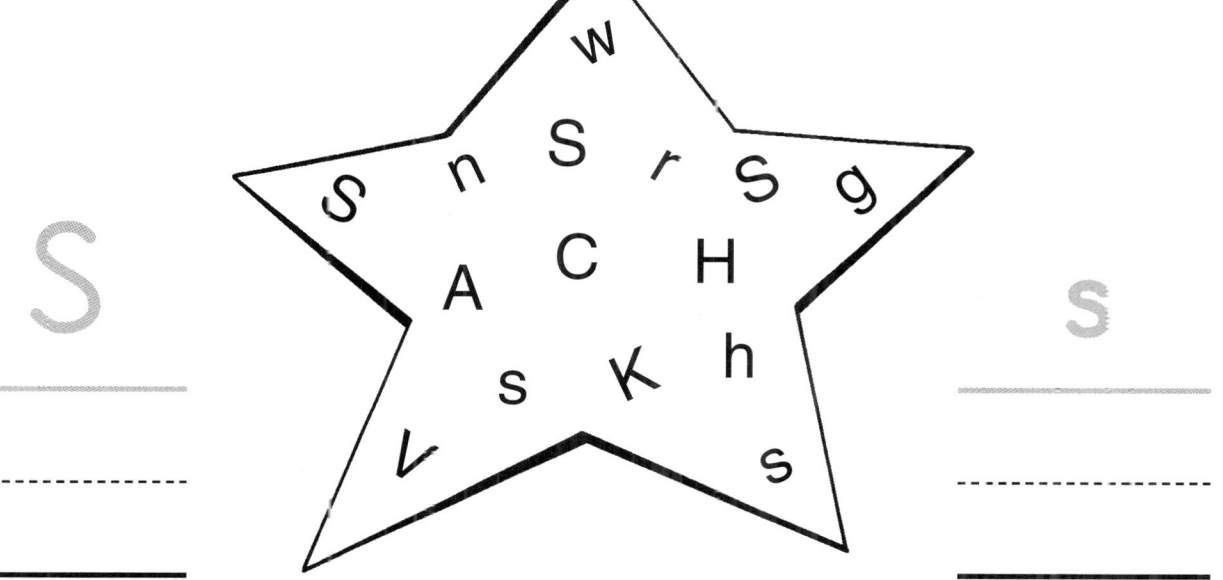

S   s

Tt is for train.

T   t

Alphabet

 a b c d e f g h i j k l m n o p q r s t u v w x y z

Uu is for umbrella.

U   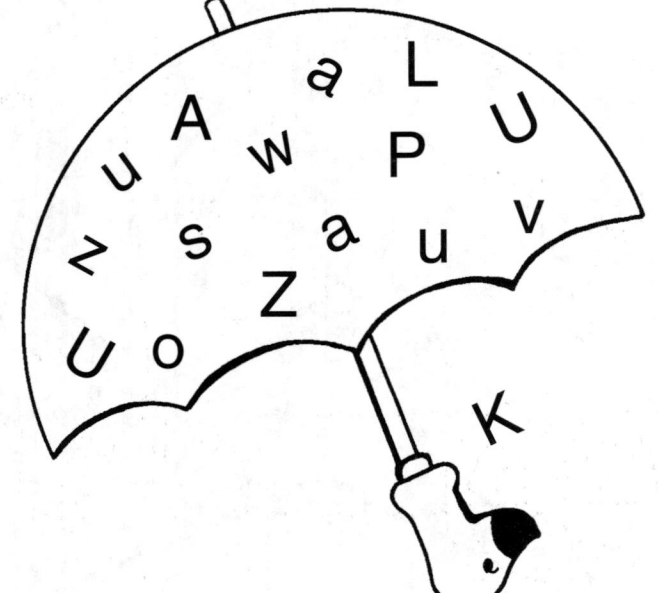   u

Vv is for vest.

V   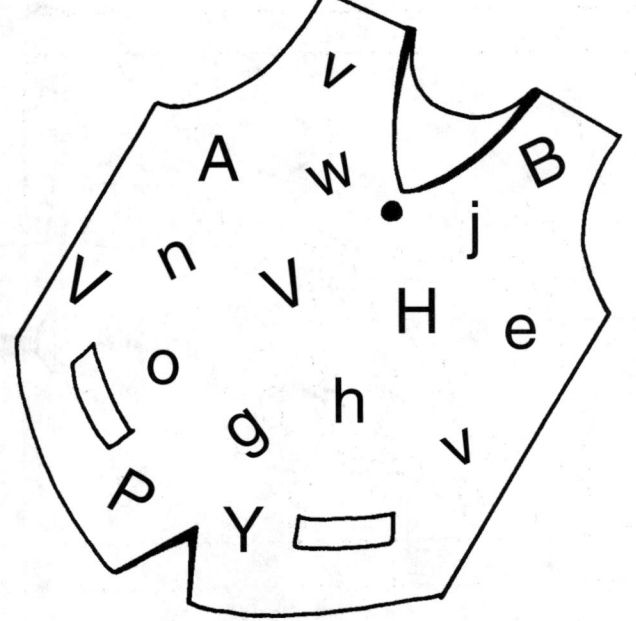   v

#3688 Skill Builders: Beginning Reading   ©Teacher Created Materials, Inc.

Alphabet

a b c d e f g h i j k l m n o p q r s t u v w x y z

Ww is for wagon.

W   w

Xx is for x-ray.

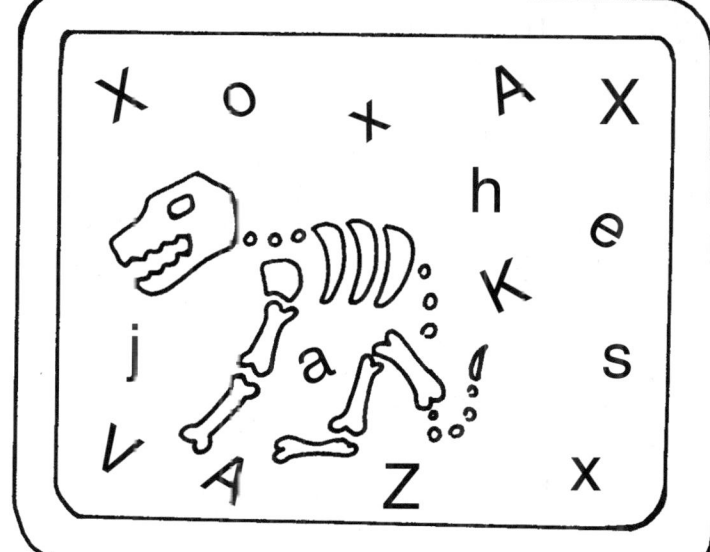

X   x

©Teacher Created Materials, Inc.   35   #3688 Skill Builders: Beginning Reading

Alphabet  abcdefghijklmnopqrstuvwxyz

Yy is for yo-yo.

Y   y

Zz is for zebra.

Z   z

#3688 Skill Builders: Beginning Reading   36   ©Teacher Created Materials, Inc.

Alphabet

a b c d e f g h i j k l m n o p q r s t u v w x y z

Fish Flashcard Games

Copy the alphabet fish flashcards (pages 38–43) onto heavy construction paper or tag board. Try using one color for the uppercase letters and another color for the lowercase letters. Cut the flashcards apart for use in the following games.

1. Match each uppercase letter fish flashcard to the corresponding lowercase letter fish flashcard.

2. Shuffle the letter flashcards and then arrange them in alphabetical order.

3. Turn the cards over so that they are face down in a square grid on the floor. Play a memory game. Take turns flipping two cards over. If they match, the player keeps the pair. If they do not match, turn them face down again in the same location and the next child takes a turn. Continue until all the cards have been paired up. The player with the most pairs wins.

4. Make an alphabet line using the flashcards. Have the children close their eyes while the teacher secretly removes one flashcard. Have the children open their eyes and decide which letter is missing.

5. Using a pocket chart and the flashcards, have the children make words using different word families. For instance, place the *a* and *t* letter flashcards in the pocket chart to form a rime, at. Place different letter flashcards in front of the rime to form words such as *bat, cat,* or *fat*.

6. Sort the letter flashcards by appearance: straight lines, curved lines, or both straight and curved lines.

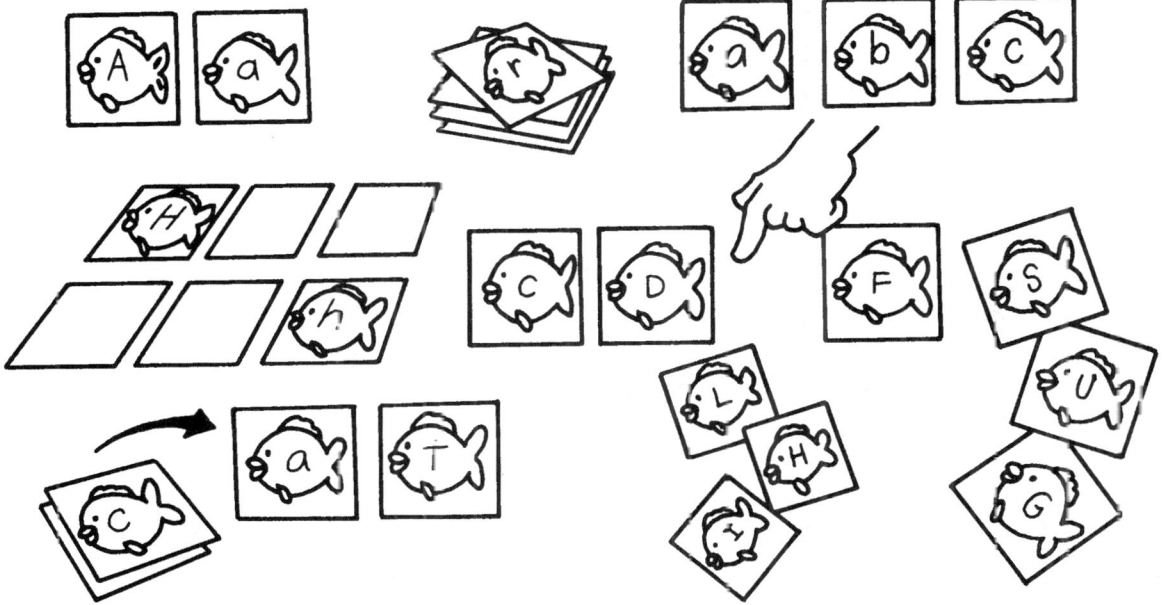

©Teacher Created Materials, Inc.   #3688 Skill Builders: Beginning Reading

Alphabet

 a b c d e f g h i j k l m n o p q r s t u v w x y z

Fish Flashcards

C	F	I
B	E	H
A	D	G

Alphabet

a b c d e f g h i j k l m n o p q r s t u v w x y z

Fish Flashcards

L	O	R
K	N	Q
J	M	P

©Teacher Created Materials, Inc.   39   #3688 Skill Builders: Beginning Reading

Alphabet

abcdefghijklmnopqrstuvwxyz

Fish Flashcards

#3688 Skill Builders: Beginning Reading 40 ©Teacher Created Materials, Inc.

Alphabet

a b c d e f g h i j k l m n o p q r s t u v w x y z

Fish Flashcards

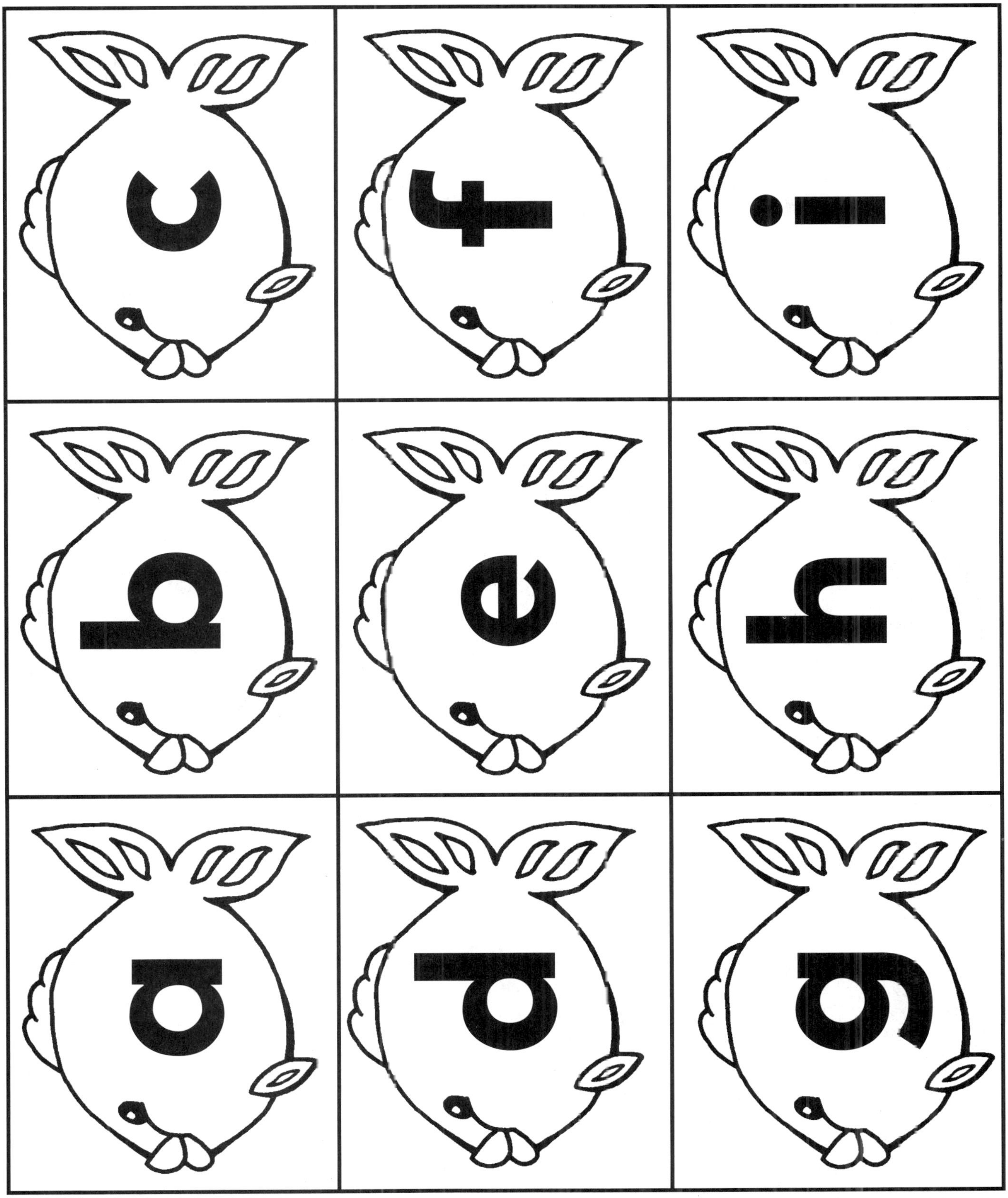

c	f	i
b	e	n
a	p	g

©Teacher Created Materials, Inc. 41 #3688 Skill Builders: Beginning Reading

Alphabet

a b c d e f g h i j k l m n o p q r s t u v w x y z

Fish Flashcards

l	o	r
k	n	p
j	m	d

#3688 Skill Builders: Beginning Reading   42   ©Teacher Created Materials, Inc.

a b c d e f g h i j k l m n o p q r s t u v w x y z

Alphabet

Fish Flashcards

u	x	
t	w	z
s	v	y

Alphabet Review

a b c d e f g h i j k l m n o p q r s t u v w x y z

Letter Cheer

Recite the following cheer with your students to practice letter sounds.

    Teacher–"Give me an 'A'" (teacher gives the letter name)

    Students–/a/ (students give the letter sound)

    Teacher–"Give me a 'B'"

    Students–/b/

    Teacher–"Give me a 'C'"

    Students–/c/

    Teacher–"Give me an 'A-B-C'"

    Students–/a/-/b/-/c/

Continue on using as many of the alphabet letters as you like.

As an extension, spell simple words using this technique.

    Teacher–"Give me a 'D'"

    Students–/d/

    Teacher– "Give me an 'O'"

    Students–/o/

    Teacher–"Give me a 'G'"

    Students–/g/

    Teacher–"Give me a "D-O-G'"

    Students–/d/-/o/-/g/

Alphabet Review

abcdefghijklmnopqrstuvwxyz

I Can Print the Alphabet

 Trace the letters of the alphabet.

A B C D

E F G H

I J K L

M N O P

Q R S T

U V W X

Y Z

Alphabet Review

 abcdefghijklmnopqrstuvwxyz

Find the Clown

 Complete the picture by connecting the dots in alphabetical order.
Color the clown.

Alphabet Review

abcdefghijklmnopqrstuvwxyz

Alpha-Bear

 Complete the picture by connecting the dots in alphabetical order.
Color the bear.

©Teacher Created Materials, Inc.   #3688 Skill Builders: Beginning Reading

Phonemic Awareness

 a b c d e f g h i j k l m n o p q r s t u v w x y z

I Hear an Aa

 Color the pictures that begin with the /a/ sound.

#3688 Skill Builders: Beginning Reading 48 ©Teacher Created Materials, Inc.

abcdefghijklmnopqrstuvwxyz

I Hear a Bb

 Color the pictures that begin with the /b/ sound.

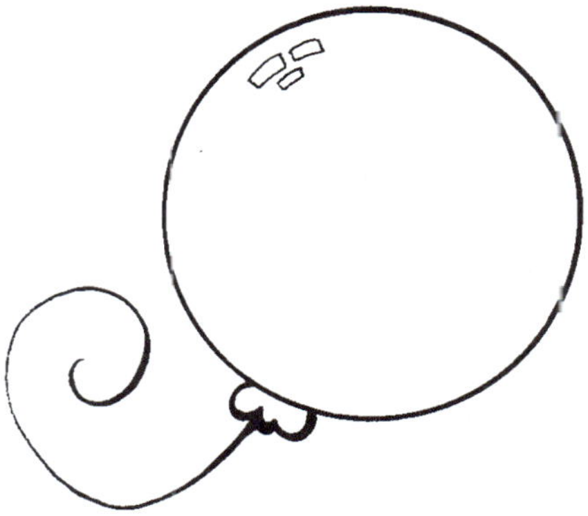

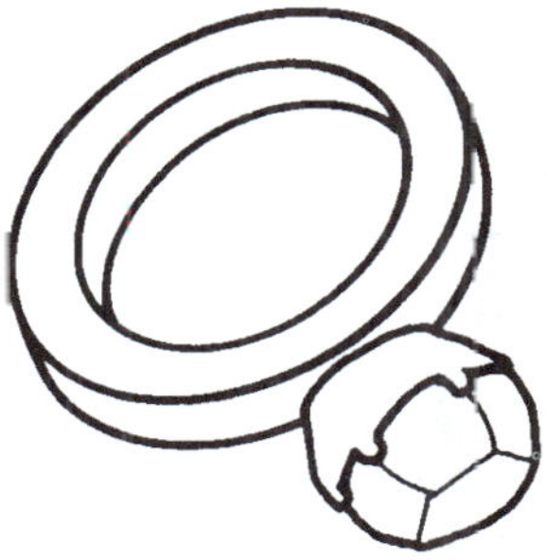

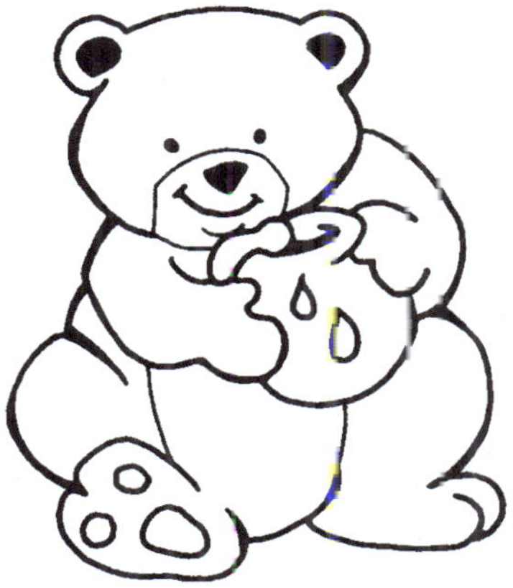

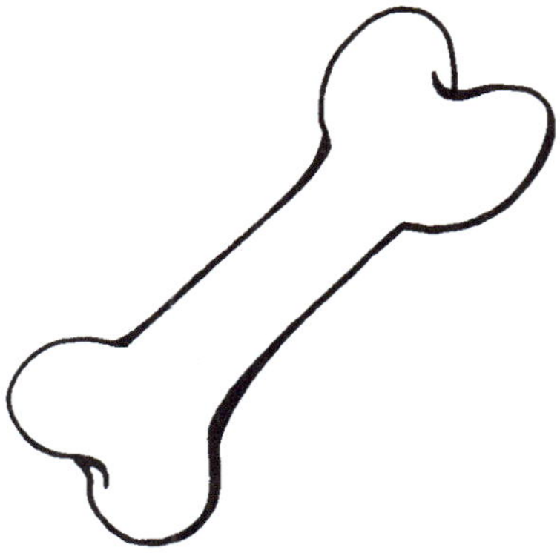

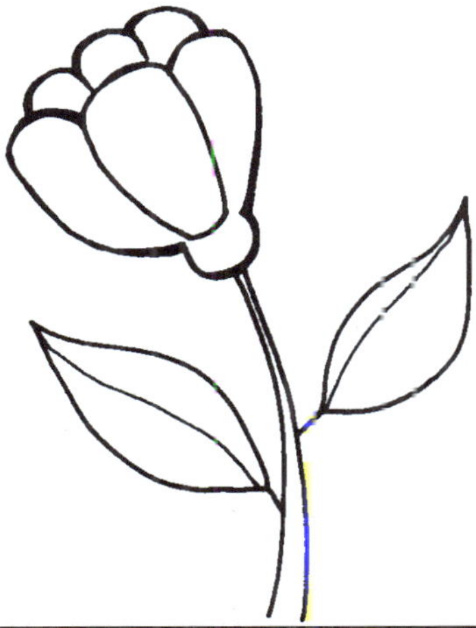

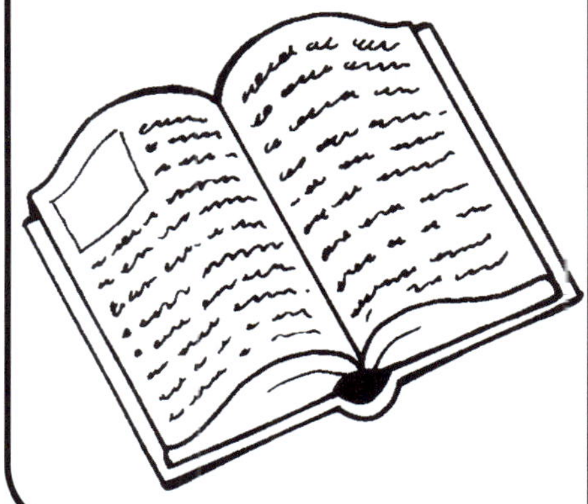

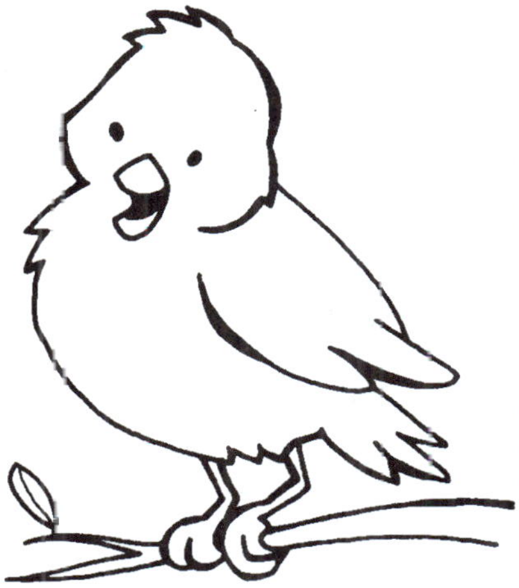

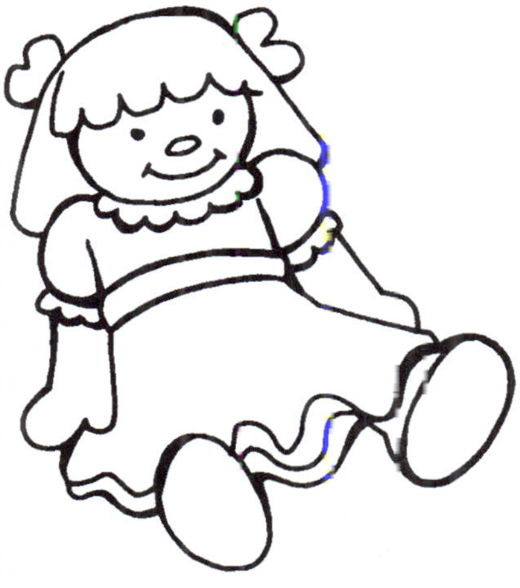

Phonemic Awareness

abcdefghijklmnopqrstuvwxyz

I Hear a Cc

 Color the pictures that begin with the /c/ sound.

Phonemic Awareness

abcdefghijklmnopqrstuvwxyz

I Hear a Dd

 Color the pictures that begin with the /d/ sound.

Phonemic Awareness

abcdefghijklmnopqrstuvwxyz

I Hear an Ee

 Color the pictures that begin with the /e/ sound.

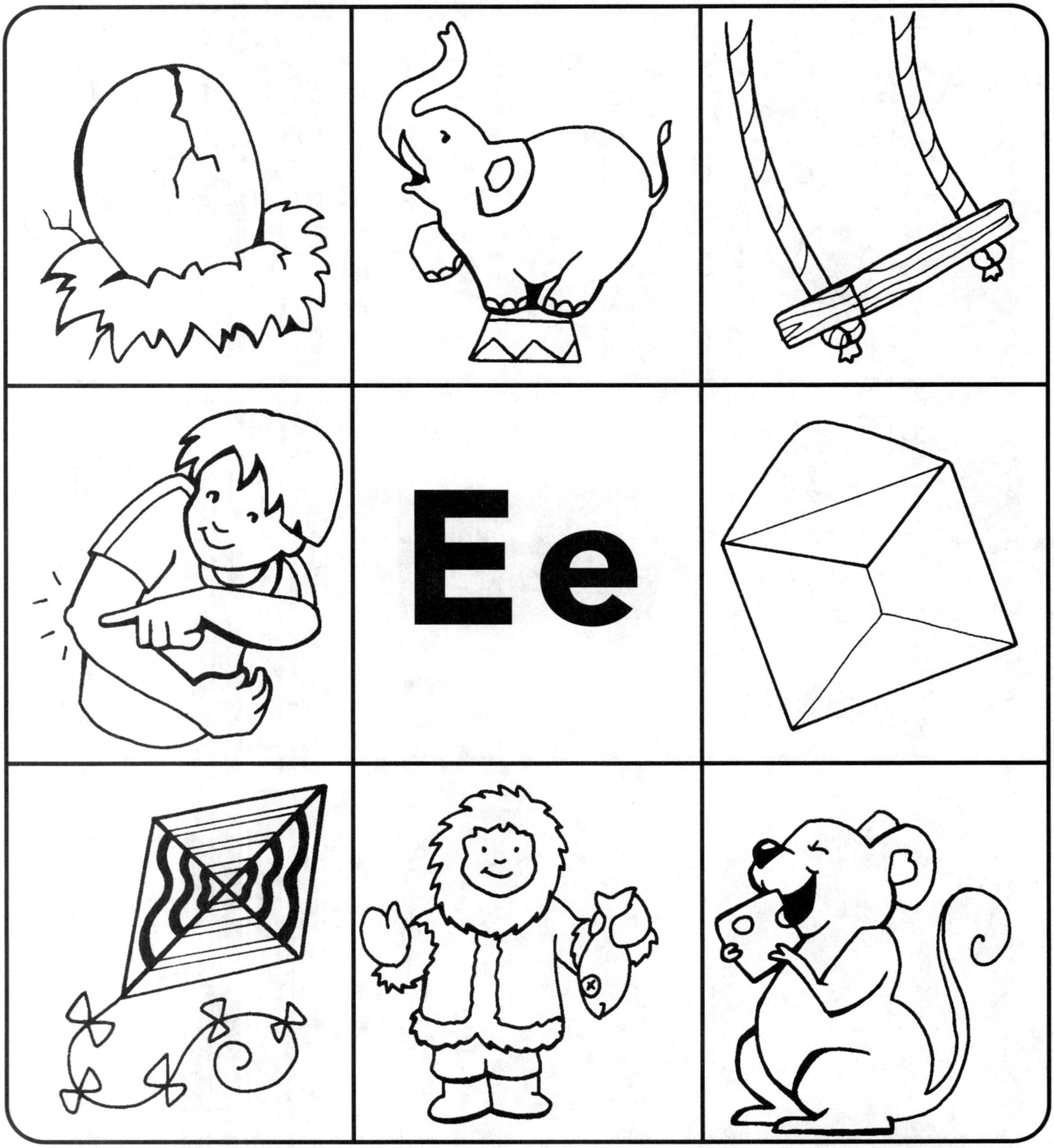

Phonemic Awareness

abcdefghijklmnopqrstuvwxyz

I Hear an Ff

 Color the pictures that begin with the /f/ sound.

Phonemic Awareness

abcdefghijklmnopqrstuvwxyz

I Hear a Gg

 Color the pictures that begin with the /g/ sound.

Phonemic Awareness

abcdefghijklmnopqrstuvwxyz

I Hear an Hh

 Color the pictures that begin with the /h/ sound.

©Teacher Created Materials, Inc. 55 #3688 Skill Builders: Beginning Reading

Phonemic Awareness

abcdefghijklmnopqrstuvwxyz

I Hear an Ii

 Color the pictures that begin with the /i/ sound.

igloo	egg	Indian
inchworm	**Ii**	iguana
tie	rabbit	umbrella

#3688 Skill Builders: Beginning Reading 56 ©Teacher Created Materials, Inc.

a b c d e f g h i j k l m n o p q r s t u v w x y z

I Hear a Jj

 Color the pictures that begin with the /j/ sound.

Phonemic Awareness

 abcdefghijklmnopqrstuvwxyz

I Hear a Kk

 Color the pictures that begin with the /k/ sound.

#3688 Skill Builders: Beginning Reading   58   ©Teacher Created Materials, Inc.

Phonemic Awareness

a b c d e f g h i j k l m n o p q r s t u v w x y z

I Hear an Ll

 Color the pictures that begin with the /l/ sound.

©Teacher Created Materials, Inc.   59   #3688 Skill Builders: Beginning Reading

Phonemic Awareness

 a b c d e f g h i j k l m n o p q r s t u v w x y z

I Hear an Mm

 Color the pictures that begin with the /m/ sound.

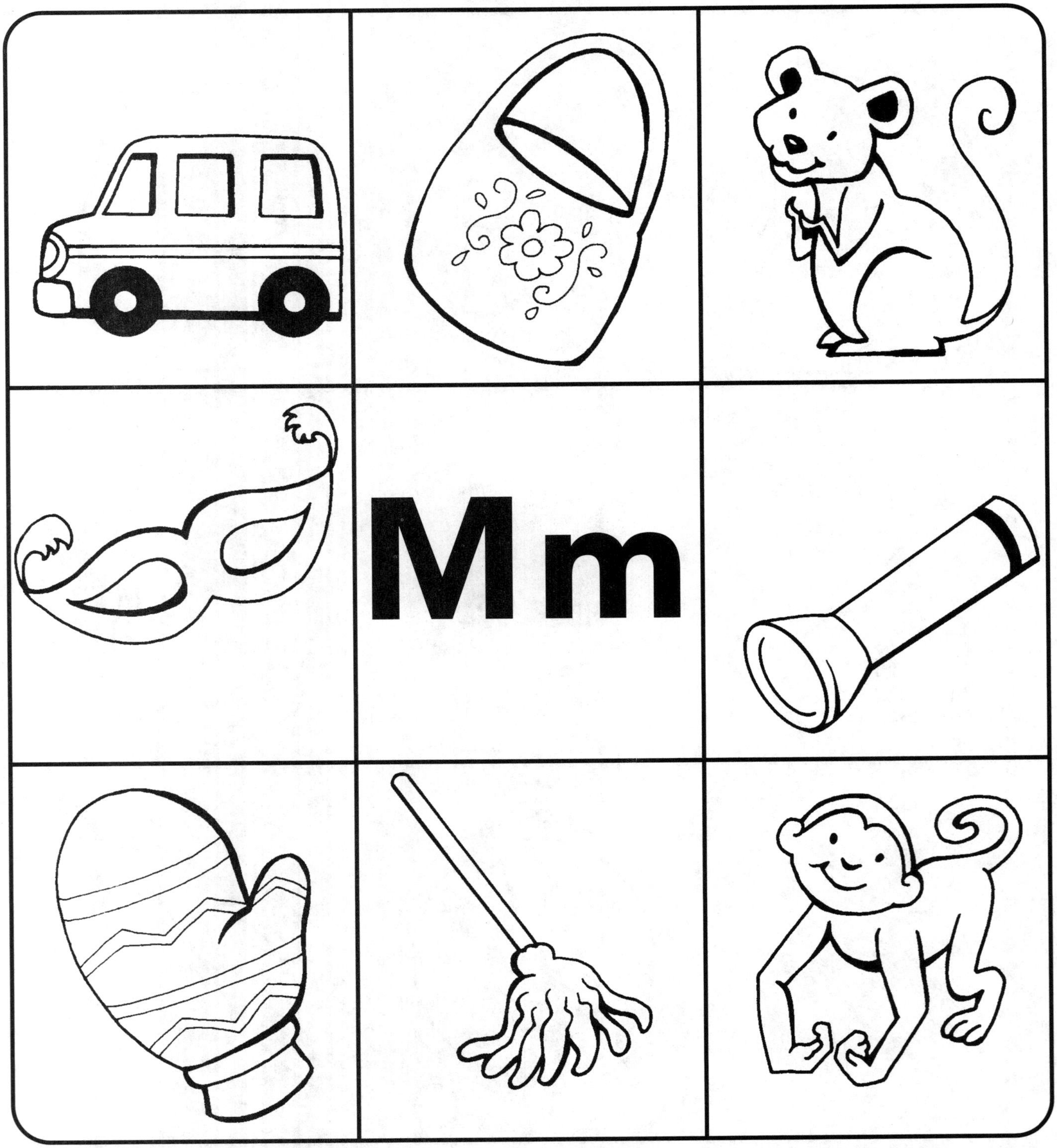

Phonemic Awareness

abcdefghijklmnopqrstuvwxyz

I Hear an Nn

 Color the pictures that begin with the /n/ sound.

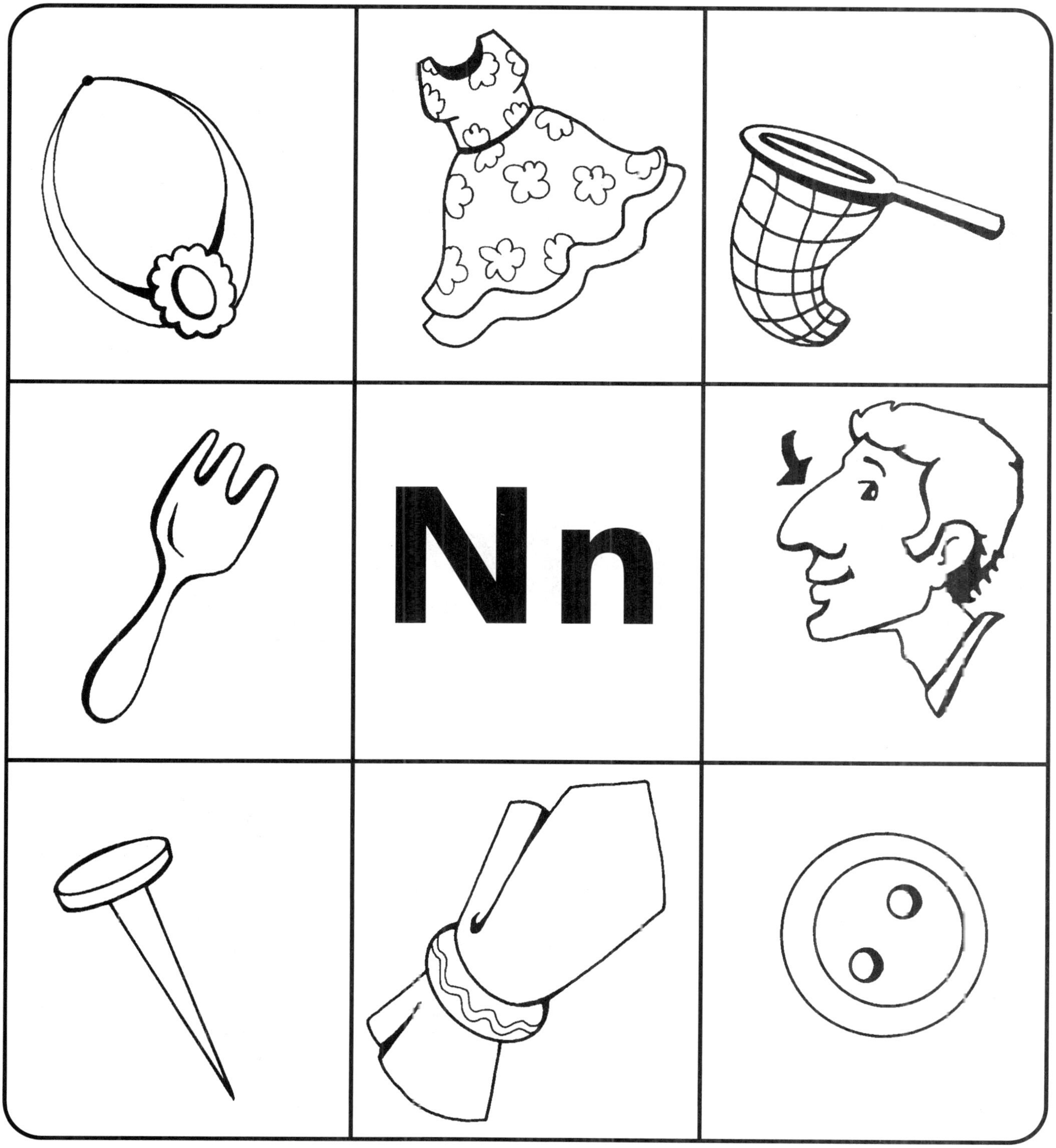

©Teacher Created Materials, Inc.   61   #3688 Skill Builders: Beginning Reading

Phonemic Awareness

a b c d e f g h i j k l m n o p q r s t u v w x y z

I Hear an Oo

 Color the pictures that begin with the /o/ sound.

Phonemic Awareness

a b c d e f g h i j k l m n o p q r s t u v w x y z

I Hear a Pp

 Color the pictures that begin with the /p/ sound.

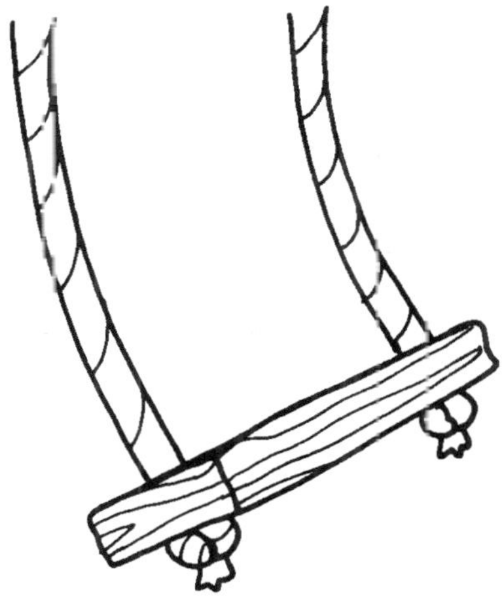

	Pp	

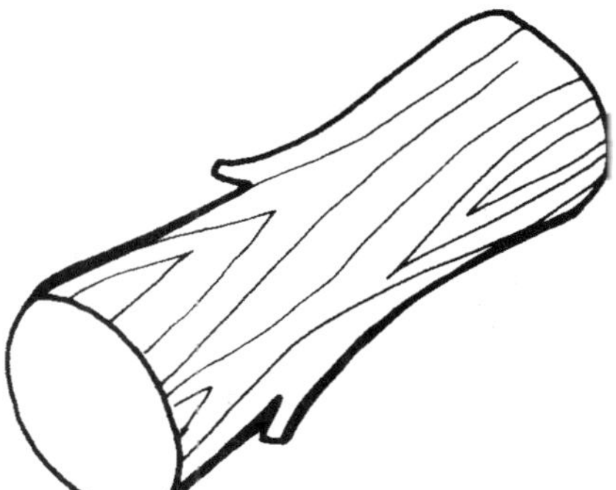

©Teacher Created Materials, Inc.   63   #3688 Skill Builders: Beginning Reading

Phonemic Awareness

 abcdefghijklmnopqrstuvwxyz

I Hear a Qq

 Color the pictures that begin with the /q/ sound.

a b c d e f g h i j k l m n o p q r s t u v w x y z

Phonemic Awareness

I Hear an Rr

 Color the pictures that begin with the /r/ sound.

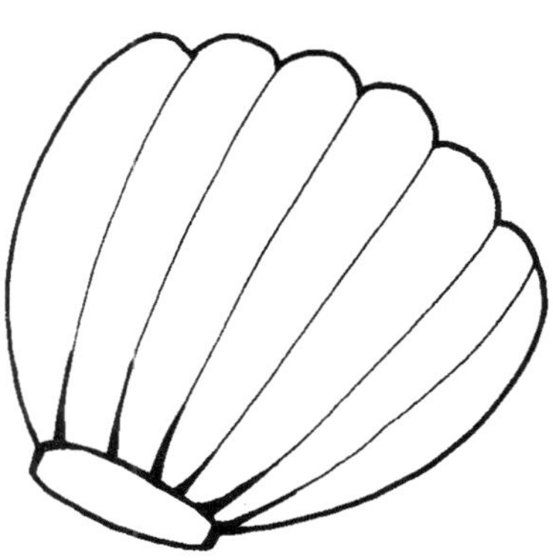

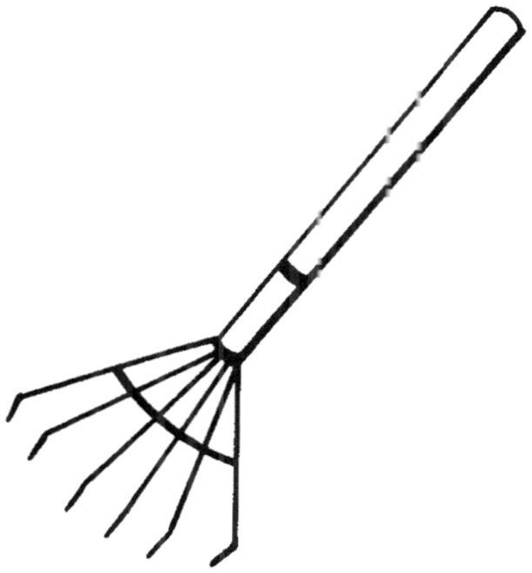

Phonemic Awareness

 abcdefghijklmnopqrstuvwxyz

I Hear an Ss

 Color the pictures that begin with the /s/ sound.

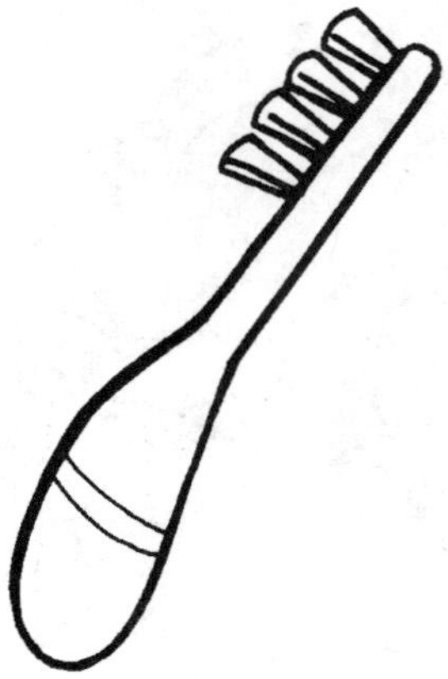

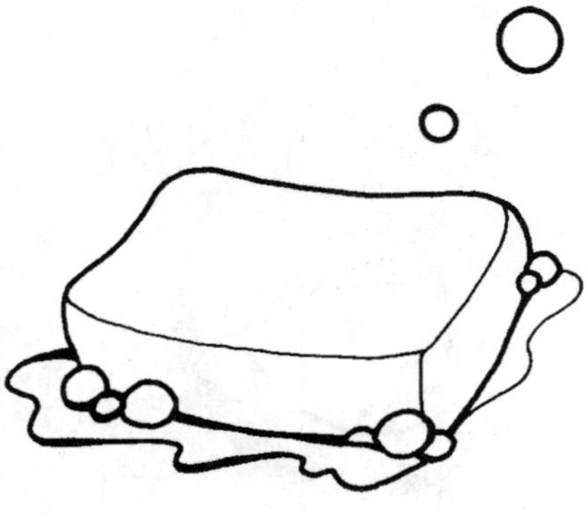

Phonemic Awareness

abcdefghijklmnopqrstuvwxyz

I Hear a Tt

 Color the pictures that begin with the /t/ sound.

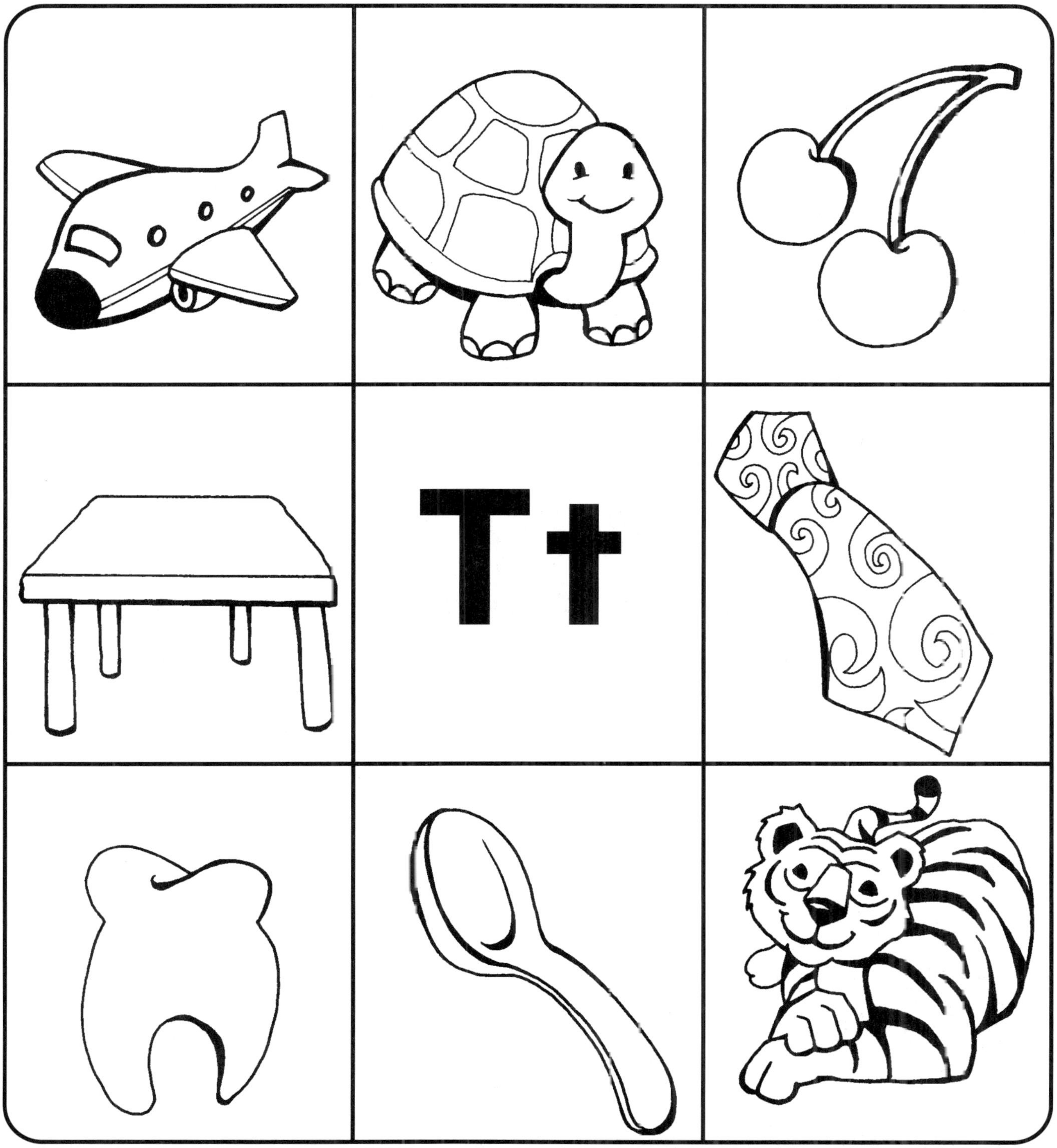

airplane	turtle	cherries
table	**Tt**	tie
tooth	spoon	tiger

Phonemic Awareness

 a b c d e f g h i j k l m n o p q r s t u v w x y z

I Hear a Uu

 Color the pictures that begin with the /u/ sound.

Phonemic Awareness

abcdefghijklmnopqrstuvwxyz

I Hear a Vv

 Color the pictures that begin with the /v/ sound.

Phonemic Awareness

 a b c d e f g h i j k l m n o p q r s t u v w x y z

I Hear a Ww

 Color the pictures that begin with the /w/ sound.

Phonemic Awareness

a b c d e f g h i j k l m n o p q r s t u v w x y z

I Hear an Xx

 Color the pictures that have the /x/ sound at the end.

Phonemic Awareness

I Hear a Yy

 Color the pictures that begin with the /y/ sound.

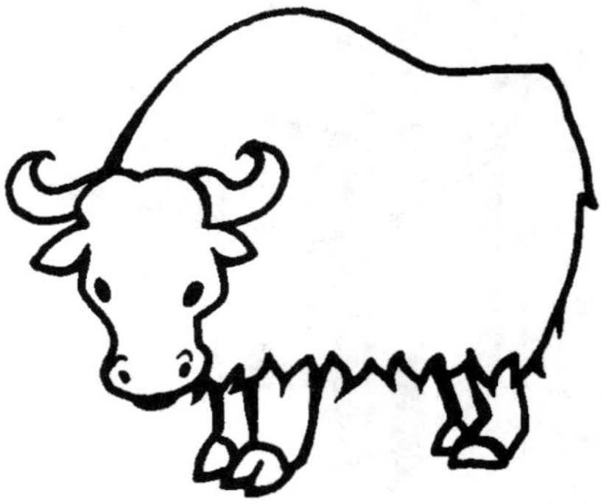

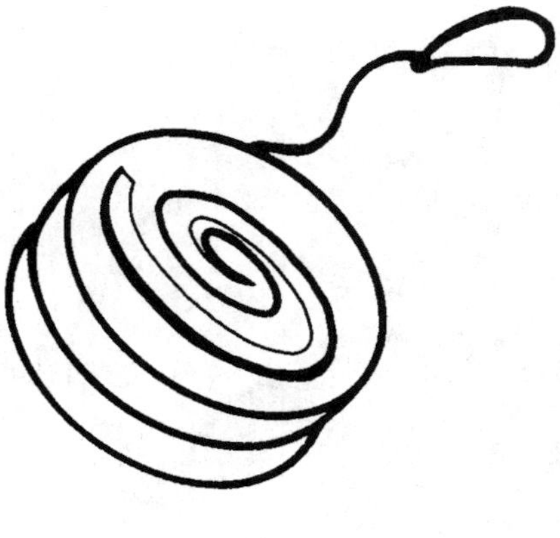

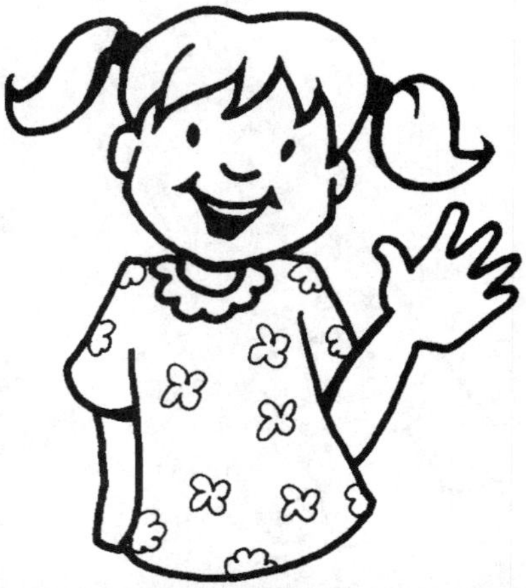

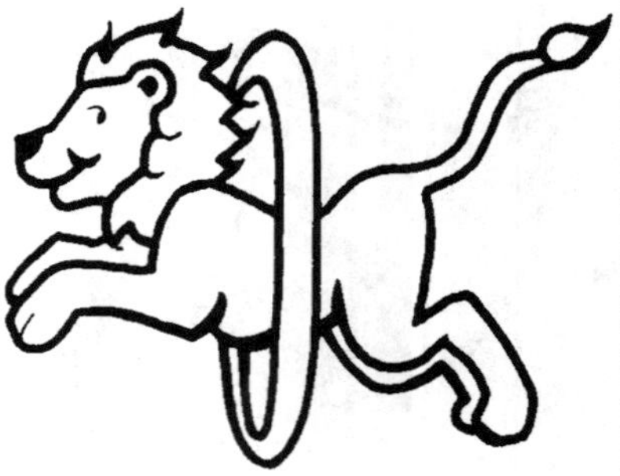

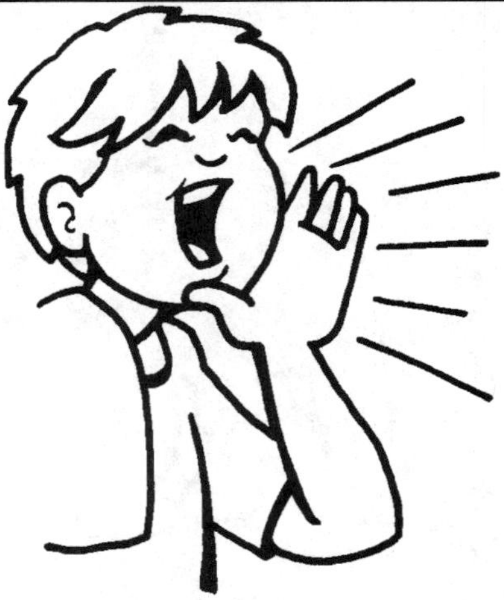

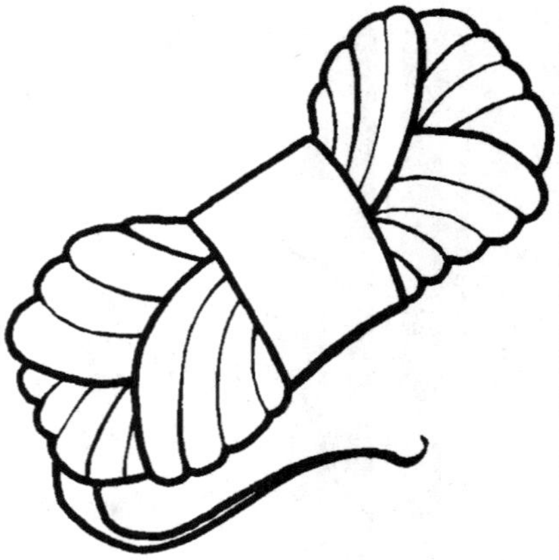

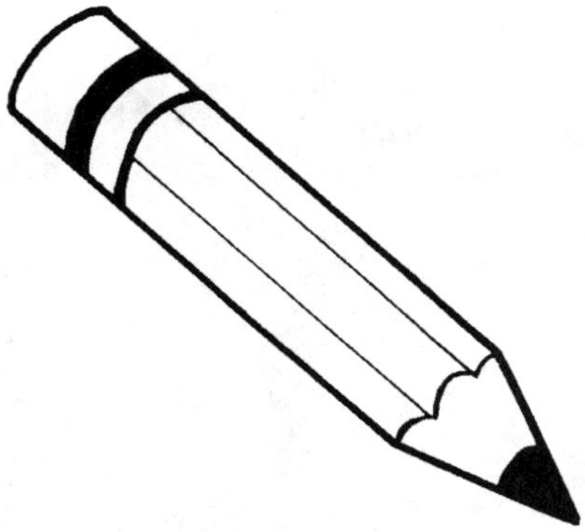

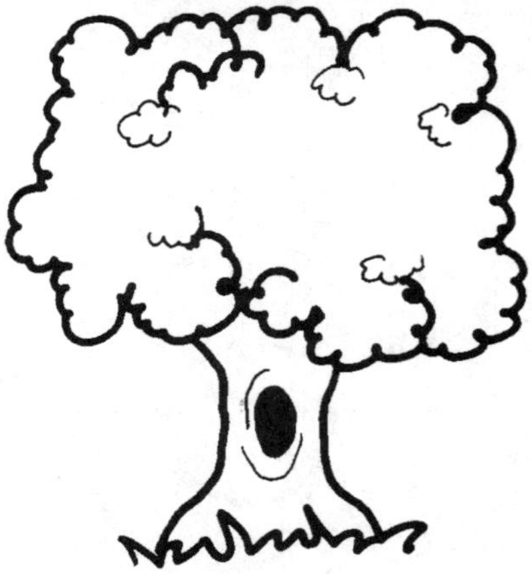

Phonemic Awareness

abcdefghijklmnopqrstuvwxyz

I Hear a Zz

 Color the pictures that begin with the /z/ sound.

Phonemic Awareness

a b c d e f g h i j k l m n o p q r s t u v w x y z

Beginning Sounds

 Write the letter that you hear at the beginning of these words.

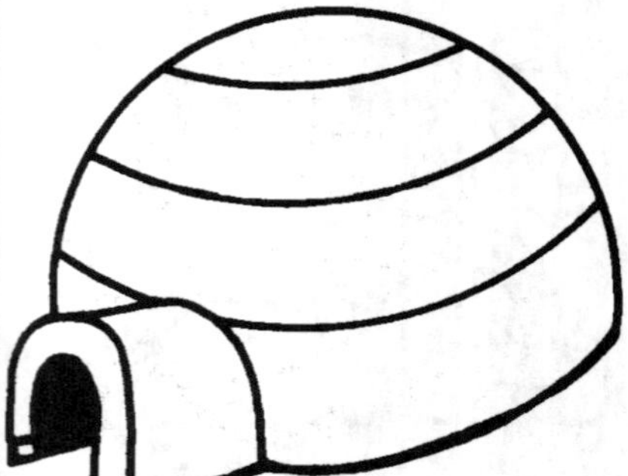

apple	egg	doll
___	___	___
frog	bat	gate
___	___	___
igloo	hat	cat
___	___	___

Phonemic Awareness

abcdefghijklmnopqrstuvwxyz
Beginning Sounds

 Write the letter that you hear at the beginning of these words.

75

Phonemic Awareness

a b c d e f g h i j k l m n o p q r s t u v w x y z

Beginning Sounds

 Write the letter that you hear at the beginning of these words.

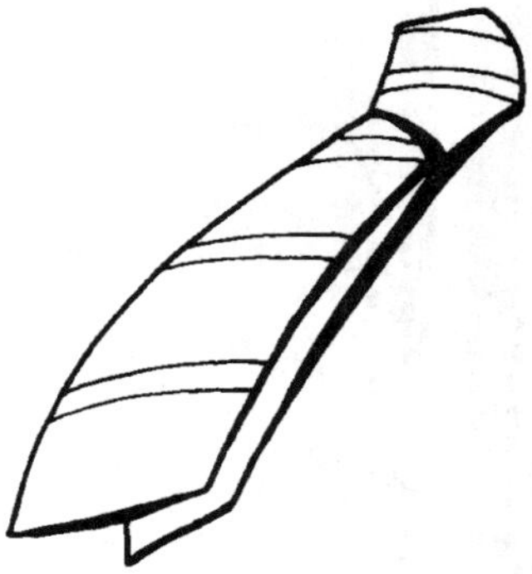

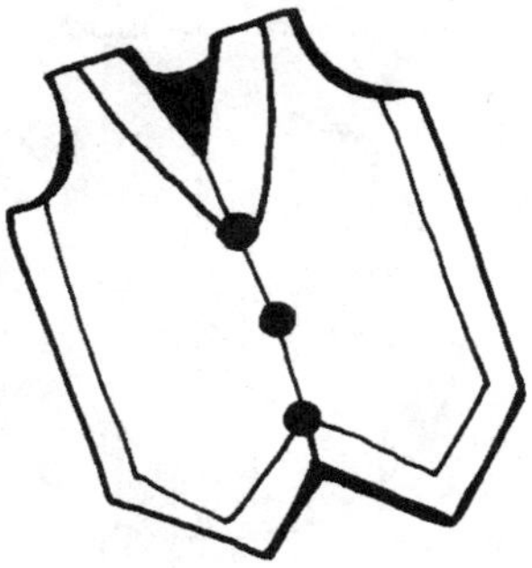

tie	zebra	umbrella
___	___	___
wagon	dinosaur (x-ray)	sun
___	___	___
yo-yo	vest	bicycle
___	___	___

#3688 Skill Builders: Beginning Reading   76   ©Teacher Created Materials, Inc.

Phonemic Awareness

a b c d e f g h i j k l m n o p q r s t u v w x y z

What's Missing?

 Complete each word by filling in the missing vowel.

c __ t	n __ t	p __ n
c __ p	d __ g	h __ t
b __ x	p __ n	p __ g

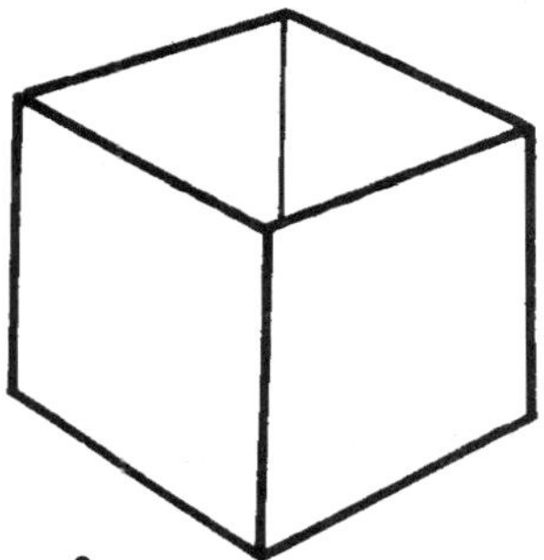

Phonemic Awareness

 abcdefghijklmnopqrstuvwxyz

What Am I?

 Circle the word that best identifies the picture in each box.
Color the pictures.

 pen pin	 cup cap
 pig peg	 nut net
 dog dug	 hat hut
 mop map	 bed bad

#3688 Skill Builders: Beginning Reading 78 ©Teacher Created Materials, Inc.

a b c d e f g h i j k l m n o p q r s t u v w x y z

Phonemic Awareness

Ending Sounds

Write the letter that you hear at the end of each word.

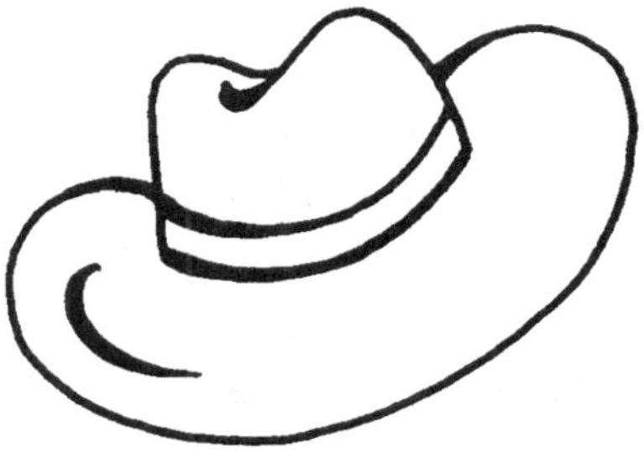

frog ___	bed ___	fan ___
mop ___	jar ___	pig ___
hat ___	fox ___	van ___

Phonemic Awareness

Ending Sounds

 Write the letter that you hear at the end of each word.

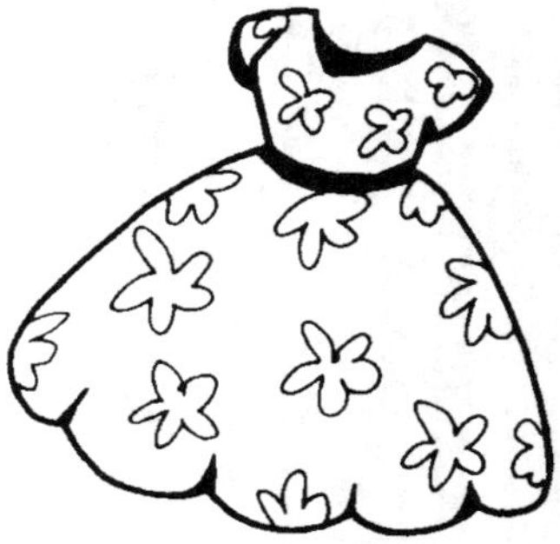

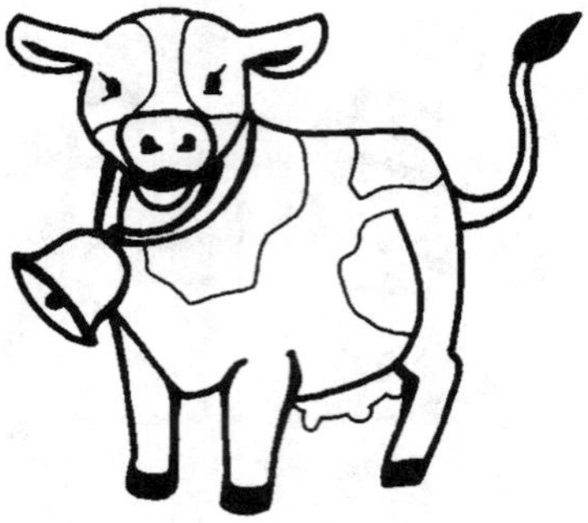

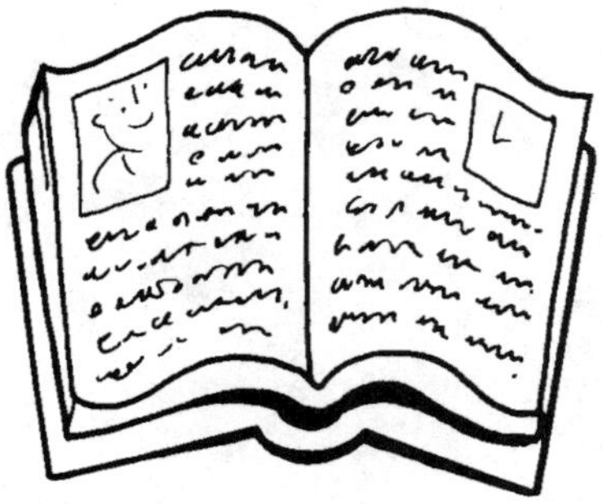

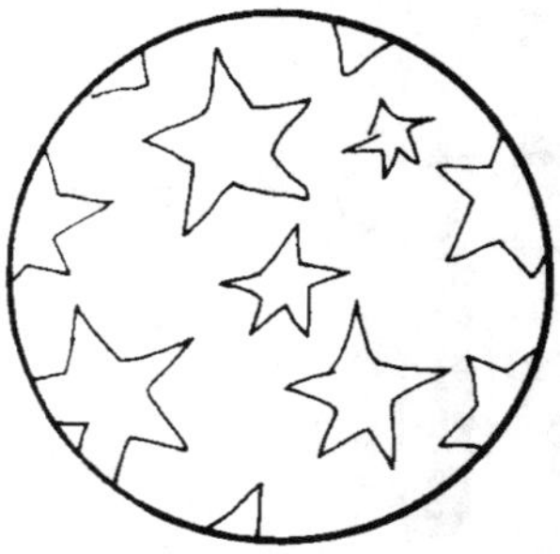

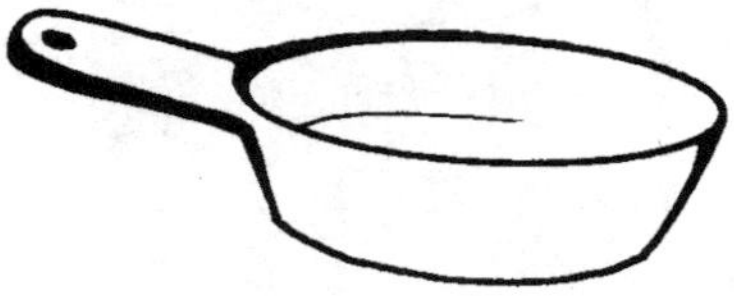

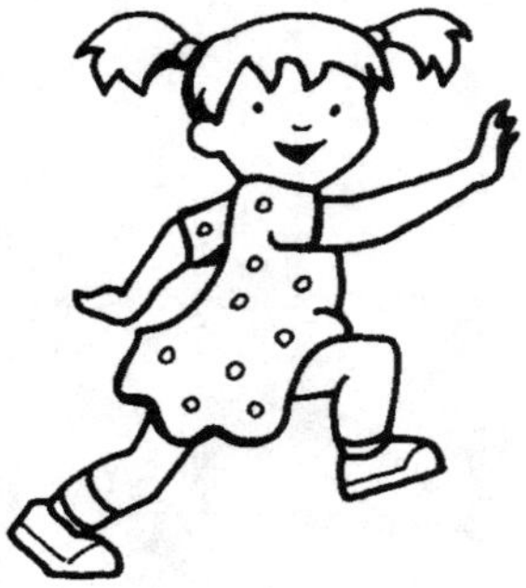

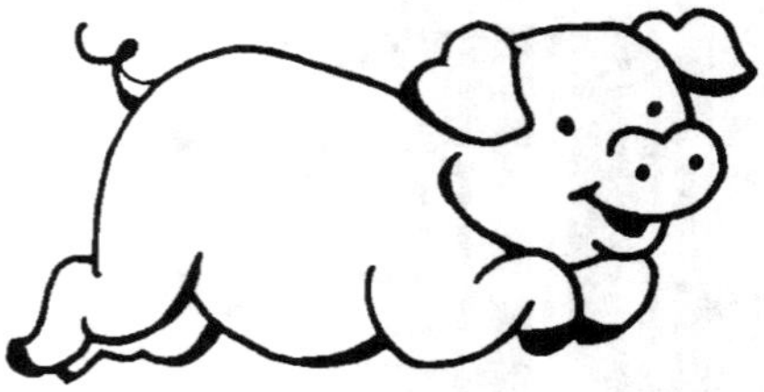

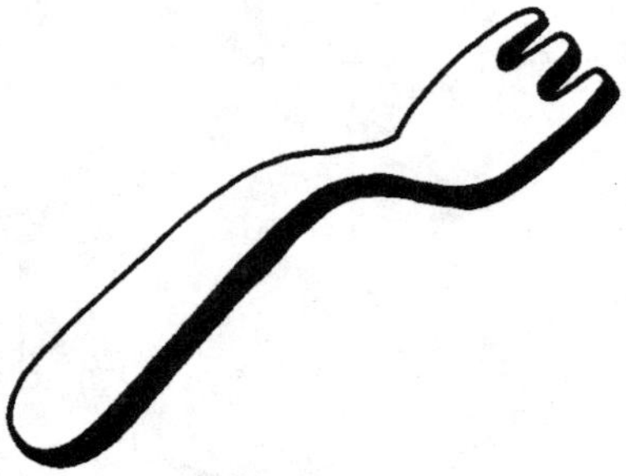

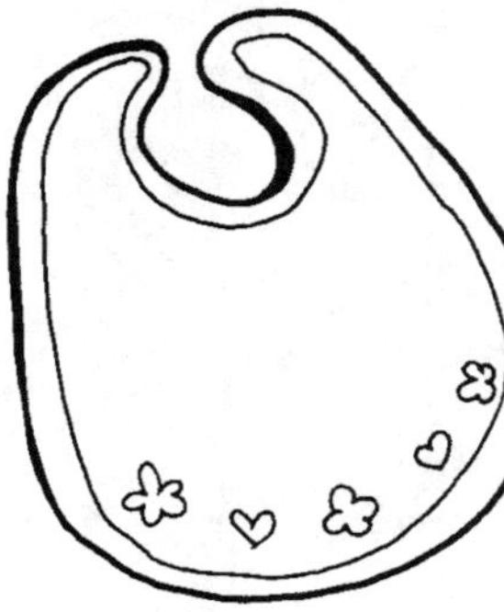

Phonemic Awareness

a b c d e f g h i j k l m n o p q r s t u v w x y z

Sound Matching

Sound matching is a component in developing phonemic awareness. This song is designed to allow children to practice and develop this skill. It is sung to the tune of "Row, Row, Row, Your Boat."

/D/ is the starting sound.

Can you make a word?

Can you tell me

When I count to three?

1–2–3 (A student is chosen to call out a word that begins with /d/.)

Repeat this using other letters of the alphabet.

Sound Isolation

Sound isolation is a component in developing phonemic awareness. This song is designed to allow children to practice and develop this skill. It is sung to the tune of "London Bridge Is Falling Down."

What's the sound that starts these words,

Starts these words, starts these words?

What's the sound that starts these words,

Apple, ant, and anchor?

/a/ is the sound that starts these words,

Starts these words, starts these words.

/a/ is the sound that starts these words.

They all start with the /a/ sound.

©Teacher Created Materials, Inc. 81 #3688 Skill Builders: Beginning Reading

Phonemic Awareness

 a b c d e f g h i j k l m n o p q r s t u v w x y z

Sound Blending

Sound blending is a component in developing phonemic awareness. This song is designed to allow children to practice and develop this skill. It is sung to the tune of "Do You Know the Muffin Man?"

> Can you guess the word I say,
>
> The word I say, the word I say?
>
> Can you guess the word I say?
>
> /C/–/a/–/t/? (say each sound slowly.)
>
> "Cat" is the word I said,
>
> The word I said, the word I said.
>
> "Cat" is the word I said.
>
> /C/–/a/–/t/ (Say each sound slowly.)

Repeat using other words.

Sound Substitution

Sound substitution is a component in developing phonemic awareness. This song is designed to allow children to practice and develop this skill. It is sung to the tune of "Row, Row, Row Your Boat."

> Row, row, row your boat
>
> Gently down the stream,
>
> Berrily, berrily, berrily, berrily,
> (Substitute the /b/ sound for /m/.)
>
> Life is but a dream.

Repeat using different letter sounds in place of the /m/ sound in *merrily*.

Syllabication

a b c d e f g h i j k l m n o p q r s t u v w x y z

What Do You Hear?

Look at the picture and the word. Say the word. Clap the word. How many syllables did you hear?

 Write that number in the space.

	dog	___
	butterfly	___
	flower	___
	car	___
	alligator	___

©Teacher Created Materials, Inc.   83   #3688 Skill Builders: Beginning Reading

Rhyme

a b c d e f g h i j k l m n o p q r s t u v w x y z

Find the Rhyme

 Say aloud the names of the pictures and color the two pictures that rhyme.

Rhyme

a b c d e f g h i j k l m n o p q r s t u v w x y z

Fun with Rhymes

 Color the pictures.

Cut out the pictures at the bottom of the page.

Glue the pictures that rhyme with the word <u>hat</u> inside the hat.

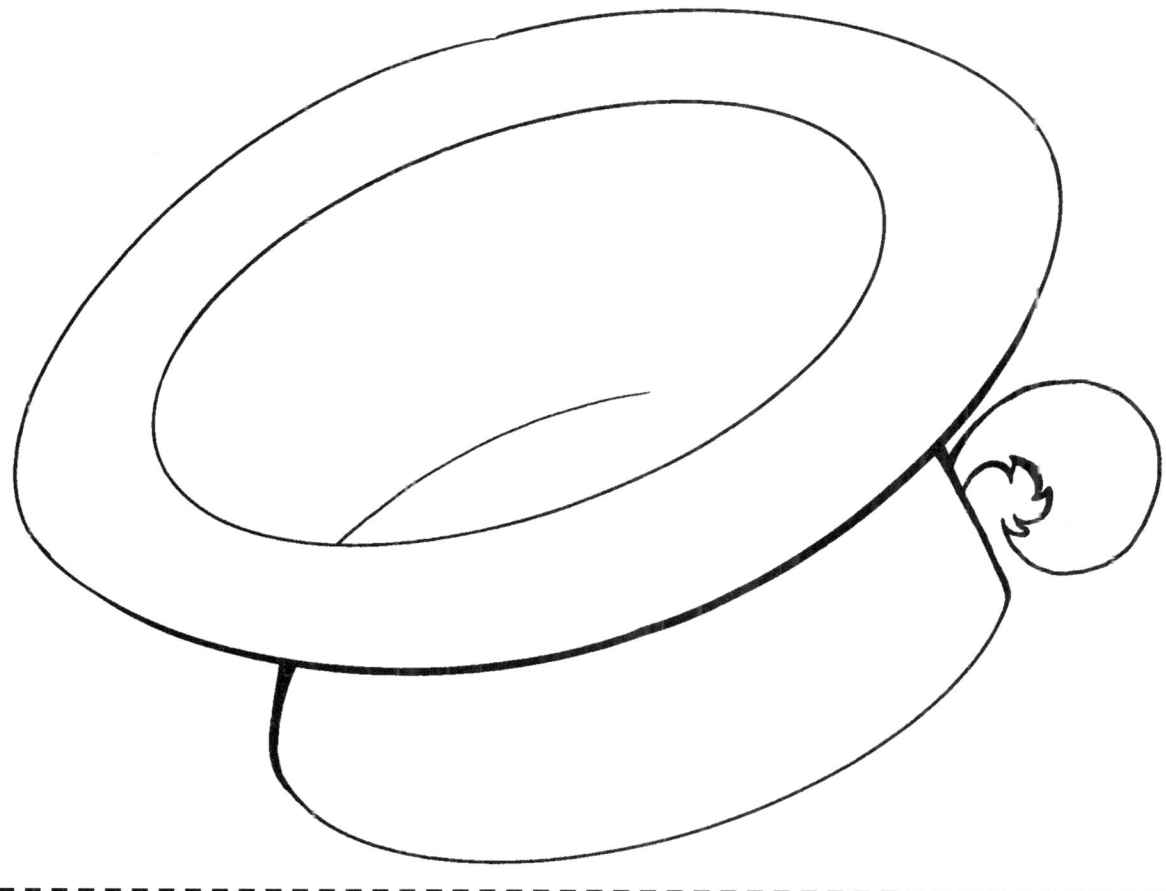

Rhyme

 abcdefghijklmnopqrstuvwxyz

Fun with Rhymes

 Color the pictures.

 Cut out the pictures at the bottom of the page.

 Glue the pictures that rhyme with the word pan inside the pan.

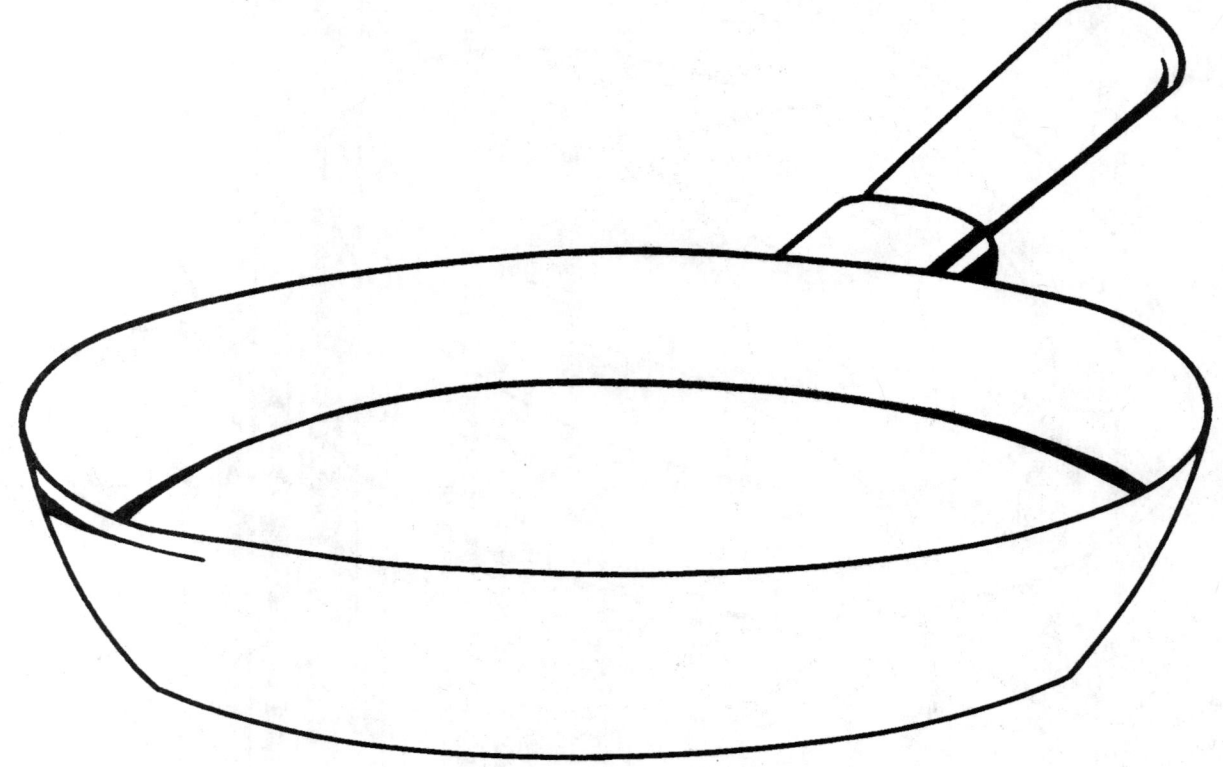

Sentence Building

a b c d e f g h i j k l m n o p q r s t u v w x y z

I Can Read

 Color the picture.

 Cut out the words at the bottom of the page.

 Glue the words into the box in the correct order.

| orange. | pumpkin | The | is |

Sentence Building

 a b c d e f g h i j k l m n o p q r s t u v w x y z

I Can Read

 Color the picture.

 Cut out the words at the bottom of the page.

 Glue the words into the box in the correct order.

a b c d e f g h i j k l m n o p q r s t u v w x y z

Reading

Color Word Book

 Cut out the color word pages and staple them together.

Color the pages and write the color words.

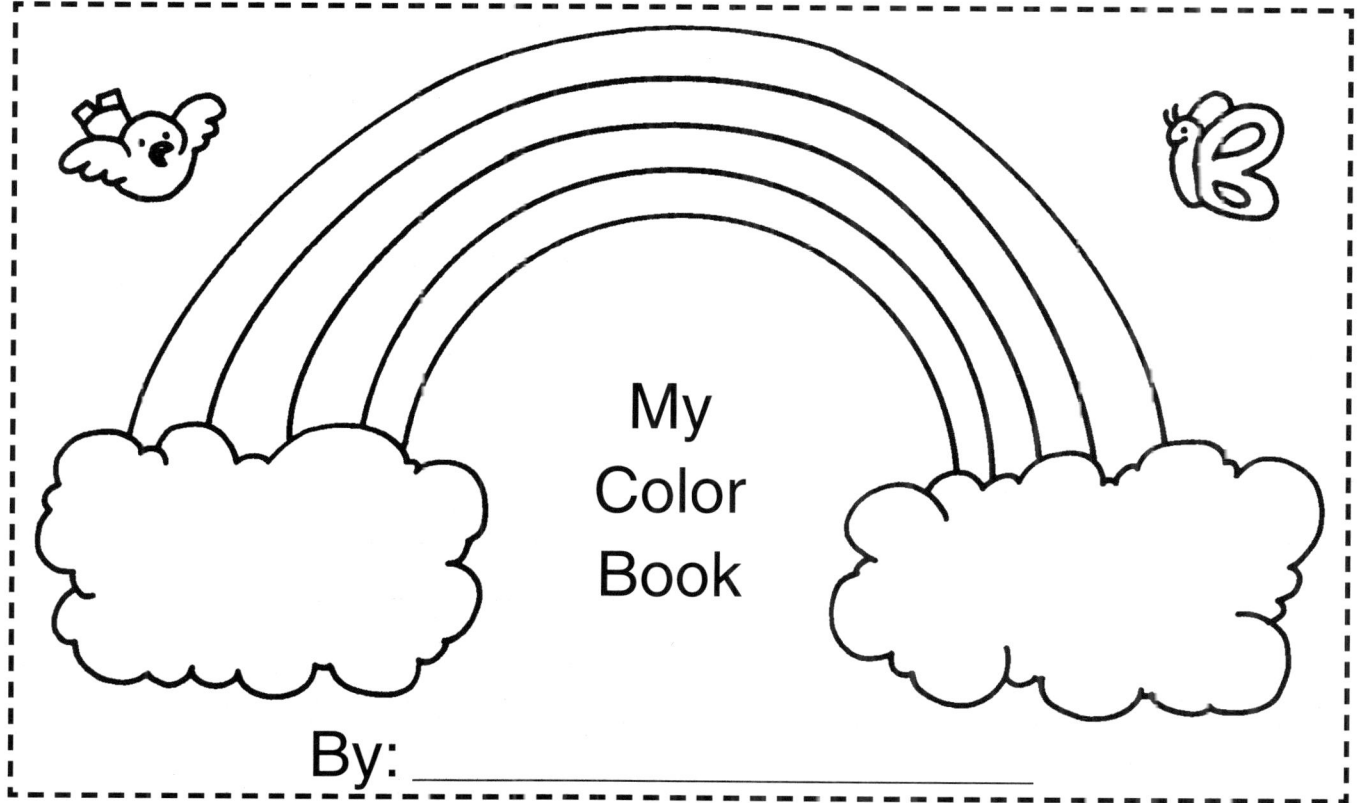

My Color Book

By: _____

Reading

abcdefghijklmnopqrstuvwxyz

Color Word Book

blue   blue

The bird is blue.

green   green

The frog is green.

Reading

abcdefghijklmnopqrstuvwxyz

Color Word Book

orange   orange

A pumpkin is orange.

yellow   yellow

The sun is yellow.

Reading

a b c d e f g h i j k l m n o p q r s t u v w x y z

Color Word Book

purple   purple

The flower is purple.

brown   brown

The dog is brown.

Reading

a b c d e f g h i j k l m n o p q r s t u v w x y z

Color Word Book

black   black

The bat is black.

red   red

The apple is red.

Reading

a b c d e f g h i j k l m n o p q r s t u v w x y z

Number Word Book

- Cut out the number word pages and staple them together.
- Color the pages and write the number words.
- Design a cover on a half sheet of construction paper.

Draw one bee.

one   one

Reading

a b c d e f g h i j k l m n o p q r s t u v w x y z

Number Word Book

Draw two snails

two two

Draw three butterflies.

three three

Reading

a b c d e f g h i j k l m n o p q r s t u v w x y z

Number Word Book

Draw four flowers.

four   *four*

Draw five ladybugs.

five   *five*